TAKE US TO YOUR CHIEF

TAKE US TO YOUR CHIEF

AND OTHER STORIES

DREW HAYDEN TAYLOR

DOUGLAS & McINTYRE

DOUGLAS AND MCINTYRE (2013) LTD.

PO Box 219, Madeira Park, BC, VON 2HO

www.douglas-mcintyre.com

Edited by Shirarose Wilensky
Copyedited by Amanda Growe
Cover design by Anna Comfort O'Keeffe
Text design by Shed Simas
Printed and bound in Canada
Distributed in the US by Publishers Group West
Printed on 100% post-consumer fiber, FSC-certified, processed chlorine-free and manufactured using biogas, a local and renewable energy source

Douglas and McIntyre (2013) Ltd. acknowledges the support of the Canada Council for the Arts, which last year invested $153 million to bring the arts to Canadians throughout the country. We also gratefully acknowledge financial support from the Government of Canada through the Canada Book Fund and from the Province of British Columbia through the BC Arts Council and the Book Publishing Tax Credit.

LIBRARY AND ARCHIVES CANADA CATALOGUING IN PUBLICATION

Taylor, Drew Hayden, 1962-, author
Take us to your chief : and other stories / Drew Hayden Taylor.

Issued in print and electronic formats.
ISBN 978-1-77162-131-1 (paperback).--ISBN 978-1-77162-132-8 (html)

I. Title.

PS8589.A885T34 2016   C813'.54   C2016-904363-0
                                               C2016-904364-9

CONTENTS

vii *Foreword*

1 A Culturally Inappropriate Armageddon
24 I Am… Am I
46 Lost in Space
56 Dreams of Doom
77 Mr. Gizmo
92 Petropaths
111 Stars
120 Superdisappointed
136 Take Us to Your Chief

147 *Acknowledgements*
150 *About the Author*

FOREWORD

Welcome to the new *terra nullius*, or as Shakespeare referred to it so well in *Hamlet*, "the undiscovered country." Or more fittingly, as stated in another classic using possibly the most famous split infinitive in history, you are about to "boldly go where no one has gone before."

A million years ago when I was a child, I was always fascinated by what could be. I think this was primarily because I was surrounded by what is and what was. As a Native person, I was constantly and importantly made aware of our heritage, our culture, everything from the past that made us unique and special. Also I was conscious of the fact that, technologically speaking, we were at a bit of a disadvantage compared to those who showed up one day for dinner and never left. I clearly remember the first time I saw television, played with a computer, got an electric toothbrush, etc. Darn clever, those white people. Native people constantly wonder at the clever innovations and devices the dominant culture feels the need to create—everything from vibrators to nuclear bombs.

Admittedly, First Nations and science fiction don't usually go together. In fact, they could be considered rather unusual topics to mention in the same sentence, much like fish and bicycles. As genre fiction goes, they are practically strangers, except for maybe the occasional parallel universe story. Many would argue that Native people are not known for their space-travelling abilities. Nor their mastery and innovation of that aforementioned modern and world-altering technology. We may have known what to do with every part of a buffalo, but how to cannibalize

viii · *Drew Hayden Taylor*

and utilize the parts from an Apple laptop to make a pair of moccasins…
the less said the better.

Many people's only contact with Native sci-fi is that famous episode
from the original *Star Trek* series called "The Paradise Syndrome," where
Kirk loses his memory and ends up living with some transplanted Indigene
on a faraway planet. These Aboriginal folks came complete with black
wigs, standard 1960s headbands and fringed miniskirts. More recently
there was the not-so-successful mixed-genre movie *Cowboys & Aliens*. But
in between, the pickings were and are lean and hard to find.

I grew up reading science fiction or, as it's sometimes called, speculative
fiction (which in itself is a controversial term, since at its essence, isn't all
fiction speculative?). First it was comic books, then television, then pulp
novels and finally what could be called the good stuff. My first serious
sci-fi literary crush was H. G. Wells. I read and reread *The Time Machine*
and *The Invisible Man* too many times to count. Discovered and devoured
the first generation of masters including Jules Verne and H. P. Lovecraft
(many consider him more of a horror writer, but I like to think he goes
both ways) and so on up through the Golden Age of Science Fiction and
into the more contemporary contributors.

To me, sci-fi was a world of possibilities. As a fan of writing, why
shouldn't my fascination extend to such unconventional works? It was
still writing, still literature in all its glory, but here they used different tools
to explore the human condition, be they aliens, advanced technology or
other such novel approaches. That was my intention with this collection
of short stories. I wanted to take traditional (a buzzword in the Native
community) science-fiction characteristics and filter them through an
Aboriginal consciousness. That is what you are holding in your hands.

Previously I dabbled a bit, sort of flirted with this concept over the
decades. In my very first play, *Toronto at Dreamer's Rock*, three sixteen-year-
old boys from three different time periods meet at the top of a magical
rock where boys have gone for thousands of years to have a vision quest.
In another play, *alterNatives*, one of the characters is a twenty-four-year-old
Ojibway man who wants to write science fiction (no relation). His partner
dismisses the genre and wants him to write the great Canadian novel, and
the drama (and comedy) begins.

I am an old hand at hybridizing. Perhaps it goes all the way back to
my DNA—I'm half Ojibway and half… not. Combining genres of writing
is a favourite hobby of mine. Over the years I've written Native comedies,

what could be called a Native magic-realism novel, a Native vampire book and graphic novel, a Native musical, and so on… Why not Native science fiction? It seemed the time was finally right.

This book, for me, is also part of a larger personal expedition in the world of First Nations writing. Part of my journey in this life both as a First Nations individual and as a writer is to expand the boundaries of what is considered Native literature. I have always believed that literature should reflect all the different aspects and facets of life. There is more to the Indigenous existence than negative social issues and victim narratives. Thomas King has a collection of Aboriginal murder mysteries. Kateri Akiwenzie-Damm has published an assortment of Indigenous erotica, and Daniel Heath Justice has written a trilogy of adventure novels featuring elves and other fantastic characters. Out of sheer interest and a growing sense of excitement, I wanted to go where no other (well, very few) Native writers had gone before. Collectively, we have such broad experiences and diverse interests. Let's explore that in our literature. Driving home my point, we have many fabulous and incredibly talented writers in our community, but some critics might argue our literary perspective is a little too predictable—of a certain limited perspective. For example, a lot of Indigenous novels and plays tend to walk a narrow path specifically restricted to stories of bygone days. Or angry/dysfunctional aspects of contemporary First Nations life. Or the hangover problems resulting from centuries of colonization. All worthwhile and necessary reflections of Aboriginal life for sure. But I wonder why it can't be more?

Now, as we're well into the twenty-first century, the time has come to explore the concept of Native Science Fiction, a phrase that I submit should no longer be considered a literary oxymoron.

It's frequently said how difficult being a writer can be. But on occasion, it is a hell of a lot of fun. Yes, so many projects are labours of love. This, I am delighted to say, was truly a labour of fun.

DREW HAYDEN TAYLOR
Curve Lake First Nation, Ontario
May 2016 (Stardate 6129.6)

A CULTURALLY INAPPROPRIATE ARMAGEDDON

PART 1

C-RES IS ON THE AIR

APRIL 27, 1991

Emily Porter was exceptionally nervous. It was a very big day, but she seemed to be the only one who cared about its significance. Aaron Bomberry and Tracey Greene hadn't arrived at the station yet, and they, too, were scheduled to begin their broadcasting careers in fifteen minutes, at high noon. Where the hell were they? This was her brainchild… Okay, maybe the other two had helped deal with the grants and the complex and mercurial powers that be at the band office and various levels of government, but C-RES had her blood and sweat all over it. If it had had DNA, it would have been hers.

The first community radio station on her reserve, one of the first of its type in this part of Canada—this was her baby. She planned to nurse it for the rest of her life. The world needed changing, she thought, and she was just the person to do it… well, at least her part of it, by providing news, weather, sports, music and talk about and for the Iroquois people of her community. Standing out on the dirt driveway, she looked up and saw the huge antenna towering above her, as if giving that distant high-flying 747 the finger. That humongous chunk of metal and wires had taken five years of rattling government and corporate offices, shaking down money, often, it seemed, pennies at a time. But there it was, standing tall, beautiful and on this bright sunny Monday, about to broadcast in 250 glorious watts the spirit of her people.

While the station was being constructed, Emily spent endless hours hammering out the broadcast schedule, the shows and hosts, the content and personnel. Now, in fourteen minutes, she and her small community would make history. It was a glorious moment. So where was everybody? Not even their brand-new news reporter was here to cover the event. Not exactly an auspicious beginning. Worse, it looked like it was going to rain. Her grandmother would have said it was a bad sign, but she also believed cats were little furry demons that coughed up hairballs on purpose.

If Aaron was in town at another movie, Emily was going to kill him. Aaron was a technical whiz. She had employed him to wire the whole place together. After that, she promoted him to radio technician. Why he would prefer the world of science fiction films to the excitement of operating a radio station, Emily couldn't understand. So as an extra incentive she had said Aaron could host a movie review show at 1:30 on Tuesday afternoons, to be repeated Saturdays at 4:00. Both Emily and Aaron knew working at the reserve radio station was as close to Hollywood as he was likely to get. Tracey agreed to the plan as long as Aaron would provide solid cinema criticism from an Iroquoian perspective—another first C-RES would achieve.

And Tracey? Hard to say where she was. The new station was almost as important to her as it was to Emily. Emily was the station manager— she loved that title—and Tracey was the program manager. She should be here to oversee the first-ever broadcast. Tracey had given up her job teaching conversational Mohawk at the local college to try her hand at broadcasting. She felt embracing new media would provide a future for her people. Since the Iroquoian languages were in danger of dying out, one of the promises she elicited from Emily was that the station would provide its listeners with weekly on-air language classes and traditional music. Emily doubted the ratings would be stratospheric, but still, it was a good thing to do. This was, after all, a community radio station, emphasis on *community*.

Thirteen minutes to go and still no sign of either. Near the chain-link fence bordering the parking lot, she spotted Karl Maracle's truck, identifiable by the dozen or so decals extolling the virtues of hunting and cats. So at least he was here... somewhere. Good old Karl—she never had to worry about him. So far.

Then, Emily saw a 1984 Toyota Corolla rolling up the long driveway. Finally! She realized she'd been holding her breath and exhaled with relief.

Tracey's feet hadn't even touched the gravel before the apologies started. "Sorry I'm late. I was doing an interview with the cbc about the new Kanien'kéha language immersion program we're starting at the community centre."

As always, Tracey preferred the correct name for their people, Kanienké'hà:ka, which translated to "People of the Flint Place," instead of Mohawk, a name given to them by white people. Tracey knew people in many of the other nations in the Iroquois Confederacy—Cayuga, Tuscarora, Seneca, Onondaga and Oneida—felt the same. When she was growing up, Emily's family had always used the term Mohawk, and Tracey was determined to break her of that, as well as the I-word. You did not say Iroquois around Tracey, only Haudenosaunee, under penalty of a withering glance and a lecture.

"This was the only time they could fit me in," Tracey continued.

Today, Tracey's skirt and patterned top were both red, her favourite colour. Even her hair had a touch of auburn to it.

"Did you mention the station? Huh? Did you?"

Emily felt it was imperative to establish the success of the station immediately. Everything in the universe must revolve around the healthy birth of the station. It was an old midwives' belief—a good, proper birth led to a good, proper life. Without waiting for an answer, Emily grabbed Tracey's arm and hurried her through the front doors and into the lobby of c-res, as in "the Res," as the employees were required to call it. Again, Emily's idea—clever, funny, punchy and memorable.

Stopping just inside the door, Tracey tried to stamp the mud off her feet—no need to destroy the new carpeting so soon—but Emily's enthusiasm would not be deterred. Dragging Tracey along, Emily made her way into the interview room, where guests would sit and chat with the DJ or host.

"Yes, I did, but there are things happening in this world other than this radio station."

"No, there aren't. Today it's radio station, radio station, radio station. Only radio station. Where's Aaron? He's late. He's very late. Aaron should be here." Emily tended to repeat key words as she got more and more agitated.

"I'm right behind you." Indeed, there was Aaron, halfway through an apple, wearing his ubiquitous Batman T-shirt.

Emily was perplexed. "I didn't see you come in."

Biting off a huge chunk of fruit, Aaron sat down with a thump in the technician's chair. "I live about a hundred metres over there, remember? I would have driven but I'm kind of low on gas." He chomped. "There a problem, honeybutt?"

Emily and Aaron had dated for two years back in high school, and he still liked to use his old nickname for her. It usually infuriated her, but then, of course, that was the point. He twisted his neck with a flick to swing his combination ponytail/mullet free from between his back and the chair.

"Geez, I wasn't sure you'd show up. And don't call me that. We're professionals."

"Yes, here I am. And yes we are." It was then that Aaron noticed the full pot of coffee across the room. For him, this was an auspicious sign. He got up to get himself a cup. "You seem kind of... excited."

Tracey nodded. "Yeah, doesn't she?"

Aaron nodded, his eyes sweeping the interview room. "We got any milk?" Coffee was not coffee without milk, be it skim, cream or Carnation. "Probably not," he said to himself. He was the only one at the station who drank his coffee with milk.

As usual, Emily was ignoring Aaron and his coffee fixation. "I hope Ontario and Canada are ready for C-RES. Eight minutes to go."

"You do realize we are just adding to the cosmic radio pollution this planet is giving off. We are like the radio-wave oil spill of the galaxy," Aaron said. The interview room, probably the entire building, was milk free. There was a farm next door, and logic suggested to Aaron that quite possibly a cow was located somewhere on the premises.

Emily was pacing back and forth across the narrow hallway, stealing glances at the clock. "What are you talking about?"

Deciding to bite the bullet, Aaron took his first sip of black coffee. It was strong and harsh, but strong and harsh coffee was better than no coffee.

"Oh, good! I get to give *you* a history lesson." He sat back down in his command chair. "Ever since Marconi and his wireless telegraph experiments, then the creation of radio broadcasting early last century, and then short-wave, television and every other method of transmitting anything, radio waves have been spilling out into space. In every direction. Travelling at the speed of light. C-RES is just going to add to that mess. Right now, solar systems sixty to eighty light-years away are receiving radio broadcasts of *Amos 'n' Andy* and *The Lone Ranger*."

Tracey said, "Oh great, now aliens are going to think all Native people talk with personal-pronoun problems."

"That's just fascinating, Aaron," Emily lied. "Feel free to mention that at the next board meeting." Why had she ever dated this guy? And why did she ever hire him?

"I'm just sayin'," Aaron rolled on, "we are joining a crowded room where everybody's talking."

Suddenly, the host of the inaugural show on C-RES brushed by them carrying a giant Tim Hortons cup. Karl Maracle was the only one of the four who actually had radio experience. Two years of college and four years of working at a small station in Mississauga had made him the station's most valuable employee. The problem was Karl was forty-six and hadn't done any radio in eighteen years.

"I hope I remember where everything is. Good luck, guys!" Karl raised both fists in an enthusiastic "Let's-go-get-'em" gesture that to Emily seemed slightly hostile. Aaron wondered if there was milk in Karl's big cup of coffee.

Behind her back, Emily crossed her fingers. It was a silly habit but a hard one to break, she knew. Tracey gave Emily a good luck kiss on the cheek, and Aaron celebrated the launch of the station by eating his apple core. "Hailing frequencies open, Captain," he added.

Emily managed to say, "Break a leg, Karl."

"Actually," interjected Tracey, "in the Native community, it's more correct to say 'wound a knee.'"

"So wound a knee!" Emily and Tracey said it together, and with a determined look on his face, Karl stepped into the sound booth for his first noon-to-four shift. C-RES was on the air!

OCTOBER 10, 1998

Emily was growing increasingly weary of these conversations. In a million years, she had never thought her station would devolve into the classic battle of ratings versus content. But it had. Emily was responsible for getting the bills paid. Tracey was in charge of feeding the souls of their listeners. But for some reason, Tracey's grasp of what could be done with a radio station never really developed beyond using it as a teaching tool. Yes, that was one of its functions, and it could be a pretty strong teacher. But people don't like to be taught all the time. People like fun and, quite frequently, to hear what the other 30 million people in the country are listening to.

"I don't know, Tracey," Emily said.

"You have to do it. We have to do it. It's part of our mandate."

"Look, Tracey…"

"I hate it when you say 'look,'" Tracey said. "I *am* looking. I'm not blind, but you might be. I know what this community needs." Today, she was dressed in a cerulean blue motif.

Sitting behind her desk, Emily sighed what must have been her seventh or eighth sigh of the morning, if anybody was counting. Already it felt like it was going to be a long day. "Maybe, but I know what this station needs."

"What do you have against the Kanien'kéha language?" Tracey placed her knuckles on Emily's desk and leaned forward in an attempt to get closer. Walking around the desk to face Emily directly might have seemed a little aggressive.

"That's a stupid question and you know it. I have constantly supported you and your cultural programming, but occasionally you, Ms. Greene, have to tune in to reality. We have your language show. We have your Mohawk—"

"Kanien'kéha."

"Kanien'kéha, then, your Kanien'kéha cooking show. Your Kanien'kéha fashion report. You've only done four shows and already you're running out of topics for the fashion show. I even let you have your specials. The one about the existential view of Kanien'kéha was actually interesting. 'I think Kanien'kéha, therefore I am Kanien'kéha.'" Emily paused in the hope that her compliment would take the edge off Tracey's stance. No such luck.

"Let's be honest, Tracey," Emily continued in a softer voice. "Your audience is dwindling. Even Aaron's Kanien'kéha interpretation of *Starship*

Troopers, the radio play, had better ratings than your latest Kanien'kéha programming. People just aren't interested in our language. And I'm talking about *our* people."

Tracey was getting tired of the truth. "So what? You want us to just play country music?!"

"Not just country music. You know we program a wide selection of genres to please the diverse audience across our community. My guess is that listening to archival drum music on the morning drive to work is probably not going to be—" Emily knew exactly what Tracey was going to say next.

"That show is not archival, it's *historical!* Either let me do it, or I will quit."

Emily waited for a moment. Should she call Tracey's bluff? "Fine! You don't have to pack up your office. You can have Sunday mornings, 8:30. Only half an hour, though."

"I'd rather have Mondays at 7:00 in the evening."

Emily shook her head. "No, I promised that to Karl for his radio bingo show. In lieu of a raise."

"But Karl's…"

"I know. But we can't cancel a show that's already been promoted. We'll just have to find a new host. So it's Sunday 8:30 or nothing." Now it was Emily's turn to wait for a response to her ultimatum.

Satisfied with her partial victory, Tracey took her knuckles off Emily's desk. She had her show. Now she had to get to work putting it together. "Thanks, Emily. You won't be sorry."

Emily already was. She hated these head-to-heads with Tracey. Somewhere back a few generations they were cousins. And Emily actually liked her cousin. Last year, Tracey had joined Weight Watchers after being diagnosed as prediabetic, and she had applied to weight loss the same force of will she brought to the station and cultural preservation. As a result, she had dropped twenty-three pounds. Unfortunately, she was short, and the added weight had helped make her a formidable physical force to be reckoned with. Now she was just short and lean. During the wet spring that year, her front door had swollen shut, imprisoning her in her own house until she phoned for help. The old Tracey would never have let an eight-by-three-foot piece of wood and glass get the best of her. Being a skinny Native woman has its drawbacks.

Emily, however, had recently been morphing into her grandmother, an imposing figure with a rather matronly physique. Running a radio station and babysitting half a dozen employees left her little time to burn calories or eat a balanced diet. She was on a first-name basis with the employees of several drive-thrus circling the reserve. Physically, Emily was now the sole alpha woman in the room and at the radio station.

As soon as Tracey left Emily's office, she found Aaron, huddled over his precious editing suite, working on something that may or may not have been for the station. He had so many pet projects that it was difficult to know what he was working on at any given time. After years of keeping the station operating, nobody questioned what he was doing because all roads, be they sound or systems, led to him. Focusing on the minutiae of a circuit board, Aaron didn't notice Tracey enter the room.

"Aaron! Aaron! Earth calling. Hello."

Turning off his headphones and shaking out his new shag cut, Aaron finally looked at Tracey.

She certainly was looking good these days, thought Aaron. "You look like somebody blew up your Death Star. What did the Emperor have to say?" After years of working together, Aaron could no longer find endearing nicknames for Emily. Theirs was not the first relationship to be altered because of hierarchical office structure.

Tracey pulled up a chair next to Aaron. "It's a go."

Aaron looked mildly surprised. "She went for it? Wow, I wasn't expecting that. This is so not her kind of show."

"You just need to know how to play her," Tracey said smugly. "First thing we have to do is find a way to digitize all the old records I found."

"Did you threaten to quit again?"

"The communications between the station manager and the program manager are privileged information," Tracey said with a full stop. "Do you think you can filter out all the scratching noises? Make them broadcast ready?"

Aaron was silent for a moment before answering as solemnly as he could, "If you bring them, I will do it."

At a garage sale put on by Tracey's cousin Joseph five months earlier, Tracey had found something very interesting.

"They belonged to Granny," Joseph wheezed due to his deviated septum. "Just found them a month ago when I was cleaning out the basement after the flood. She left them to me when she died. I didn't know what to do with them. Interested?"

Tracey didn't want to show how interested she was. Stacked in two beat-up boxes were countless thick polyvinyl slabs of Haudenosaunee culture. Sometime in the 1920s, an anthropologist had come to their village seeking to record traditional songs of their people. He graciously made copies and sent the records back to their grandmother as thanks for her help. Authentic, vintage and original Haudenosaunee social songs and, with any luck, specifically Kanienké'hà:ka ones. c-RES listeners and the world had to know about these.

Tracey could dimly remember her grandmother playing the records while she babysat Tracey and her cousins. Occasionally, snatches of the songs would creep out of her subconscious like the faint aroma of some delicious pastry made by a loved one long ago. As soon as she found the records, she knew this new way of generating more interest in her people's heritage was practically heaven sent. Now that Emily was no longer the main stumbling block, she could put a program together that truly show-cased the traditional songs of her people. It might even foster more unity within the Iroquois Confederacy, not to mention placing another brick in the dam that held back the flood of the dominant culture's influence. c-RES—all social music, all the time was her motto.

A few minutes later, lugging the treasured boxes into Aaron's sound lab, a place he liked to call his "magic suite," Tracey was ready to start immediately. At that point he was huddled over a non-responsive and ancient Ampex reel-to-reel recording machine. His curiosity piqued by her story, Aaron stopped his labours long enough to rifle through Tracey's precious box of records. A look of concern popped up on his face.

Tracey noticed it instantly. "I know that look. What's wrong?"

"My bad. I… these records…" He took a deep breath. "These are 78s—I didn't realize when you said records they would be these old, massive hunks of wax."

"Why is this a problem?"

Leaning back, Aaron stared at the box, but his mind was elsewhere, already working on rectifying the problem. "They may just take a little more time. I think I have one of those old-time record-player arms that can handle these artifacts. Give me a second." He started to rummage around in a large box full of what appeared to Tracey to be vintage tech equipment.

Tracey was amazed. "You have one of those? In here?" She had heard rumours that Aaron had UFO odds and ends that had been rescued from Roswell hidden somewhere in the labyrinth of his office.

Finally, she heard an "Aha!" as Aaron's head and right arm emerged from the crate, victoriously holding a large metallic device. It reminded

Tracey of the arm that had been on the record player she had owned as a teenager, except this was much larger and more ornate.

"Never throw anything out. That's my rule."

Aaron, the problem solver, had come through for her once again. Already he was busy attaching it to a worn stereo.

"It'll just take a second," he said, grabbing his soldering iron.

Tracey leaned against a counter and looked around the room, wondering what other marvels were lurking in bins and shelves. All around the half mixing/editing, half repair room was a hodgepodge of wires, circuit boards, equipment and tools. An altar to man's insatiable need to tinker and invent. It looked like a Terminator had exploded in here, which suited Aaron's aesthetic just fine.

A few minutes passed before he spoke again. "There."

The confidence and finality in how Aaron said that single word gave Tracey hope that she and her community might actually be able to hear what was on the records she cradled so protectively.

"Let's take another look at those babies," Aaron said. Once more, he began leafing through the contents of the box. "I haven't heard of half of these songs. You sure they're authentic?" Aaron's great-aunt was a clan mother, so he was no stranger to the songs of his people.

"Of course they are. I've researched and double-checked as many as I could. I can't tell you how cool this is! Look, one of the earliest recordings of 'The Alligator Dance' known. Same with 'The Smoke Dance' and 'The Pigeon Dance.' This is priceless."

The Haudenosaunee people were well known for a variety of social dances and songs, usually sung with a unique water drum. Who knows? She might get one of those Aboriginal Achievement Awards for her show.

Aaron was holding up one record, studying the worn and faded wording on the label at the centre. "I've never heard of this one… 'The Calling Song'?"

"Me neither. I looked everywhere. It seems to have disappeared sometime between when it was recorded and now." Unfortunately, that applied to a lot of Haudenosaunee and other First Nations cultural offerings in the New World. Segments of precious history lost in the progression of Manifest Destiny. But moments like this made her feel there was hope. "Can you play it?"

"Can and will do. Actually, this is kind of exciting. A lost archive of mysterious records containing unknown songs. A very Indiana Jones kind of thing."

"Just play the song." Tracey's pulse quickened.

Try as he might, Aaron couldn't get rid of all the scratching sounds loved by vinyl fans. Then, faintly, a water drum could be heard, reminding Tracey of the sound of a heartbeat, specifically a baby's heartbeat but at an even higher rate. The rapid succession of thump-thumps echoing back from the water in the drum was the sound every Haudenosaunee knew and was proud of. The sound gradually built. The rising volume of the water drum was followed by growing voices that sounded like a dozen Haudenosaunee elders singing in unison. The song seemed to have all the characteristics of a traditional social melody, but then it grew increasingly discordant. Each voice seemed to find dominance over the next, as if the elders were proclaiming their place in the universe. The discord lasted a couple more minutes before returning to the more familiar keen of the traditional social song. Slowly the voices ebbed away, leaving the water drum. Then there was a scratchy nothing before the sound of the needle being lifted. Aaron turned the machine off.

"Well, that was interesting. No wonder it didn't catch on. What do you make of that?" Aaron asked. As if Tracey had any idea.

She was silent for a moment, letting the vestiges of the sound slowly evaporate from her mind. "It was very different. Most of our songs have a purpose or a meaning. What did the label of the record say it was again?"

"'The Calling Song,'" Aaron said. "Maybe if you're looking for a moose!"

Tracey gave Aaron a quick swat on the back of his head. "Be respectful."

"Always," Aaron gave back. "Are you really going to broadcast it? It's worse than a Klingon opera." Grabbing his big mug of coffee with his left hand, he handed the record back to Tracey with his right. "I mean, I can clean it up all you want, but really… You think people will want to listen to that? I mean, I'm as proud of our culture as the next Mohawk—"

"Kanienké'hà:ka!"

"Kanienké'hà:ka, then, but that sure ain't our best work."

Tracey had to agree. "It would be a bit intense first thing in the morning."

She knew this song had to have some significance. It came from her community, so maybe somebody in the listening audience might know.

"Still, it's our heritage." Tracey's imagination and enthusiasm ran on. "I mean, it's a previously unknown social song. Do you know how important that is? Maybe what we should do…" Her mind was still whirling.

"Maybe we should put it in heavy rotation and run a contest for the best information leading to the meaning of 'The Calling Song'!"

Realizing his mug was empty, Aaron stood to adjourn to the interview room. "That might work. Look, I'll do what you want, but I'm predicting a disaster."

"Disaster? You're being overdramatic," Tracey scoffed. "What's so disastrous about this song?"

"Oh, any number of things. We don't know if it's authentic. We just have the word of a long-dead cultural anthropologist. And you know how considerate they were. It doesn't sound like any other social song we know. You might just be setting yourself up to fail. And," he paused for dramatic effect, "I don't like the song. Makes me uncomfortable."

"Don't worry," Tracey said. "It'll be a great mystery for the community to solve!"

Knowing it was futile to even attempt to dissuade her, Aaron asked the bigger question as he walked out the door. "Hey Tracey, can I get a ride with you to Karl's funeral tomorrow?"

DECEMBER 17, 2018

Emily, Tracey and Aaron huddled around the television in the interview room, watching the special report coming from the CBC news network. They hadn't moved in almost twenty minutes. Movement took premeditated thought and choice, and all free will had been stolen by the television. If a CD of Robbie Robertson hadn't been playing, there would have been dead air emanating from the C-RES antenna.

"Do you think...?" Emily ventured.

"Shh!" Aaron wanted no interruptions while he soaked up what was the most amazing event in recorded history. Barely registering Aaron's rebuke, Emily placed one hand over her mouth at what she was witnessing. Tracey's knuckles turned white as she gripped the table, still dusted with sesame seeds from bagels and doughnut sugar. Aaron found the remote and turned up the volume.

"It has been confirmed. It appears there is life beyond Earth, and it is on its way here. Earlier today, in a joint press conference, a panel of world leaders combined with representatives from NASA, SETI and various other space exploration organizations announced the approach of what appears to be a large spaceship originating beyond our solar system. At the moment, it is located somewhere between the orbits of Saturn and Uranus, approaching at approximately fifty-two kilometres a second. Officials are either reluctant or unwilling to speculate on the origins of the large ship, estimated to be over four miles wide. Needless to say, the world and its political, religious and scientific leaders are furiously discussing the implications for the people of Planet Earth of such an event, which we are now referring to as 'contact.' In an attempt to communicate, greetings in all known languages have been broadcasted to the approaching ship."

"Betcha not in Kanien'kéha! They always leave us out, goddammit."

Emily rolled her eyes. "Give it a break, Tracey."

Almost inaudibly Aaron breathed, "*Independence Day.*"

"What?" snapped Emily.

"A movie. Shh."

"The Pope and the leaders of all major countries have called for calm. As the alien ship moves closer, we are all wondering if this will be the greatest event in Earth's history or perhaps the most tragic. It seems we are fated to find out. For more background—"

Emily muted the television, prompting protests from the other two. "Be quiet, both of you. We should really get on the air with this."

There was a moment of silence as Emily's suggestion worked its way into their cerebral cortices.

Tracey was deep in her own political meltdown. "Did you hear what they're calling it? 'Contact.' Does that sound familiar to either of you? Man, I bet both sides already have people drawing up treaties." She was practically yelling. "But now the shoe is on the other foot, isn't it? The more things change, the more they stay the same. That should be our lead story!"

Aaron gesticulated wildly at the television. "Spaceships! Spaceships?! Turn it back on!"

Emily would not be deterred. "Don't you see? This is our chance to shine. Let's take this story and run with it!"

Tracey was nodding vigorously. "I agree. I think one 'contact' is enough in any culture's existence, don't you? Let's get a panel together of clan elders and—

Once again, Aaron felt the need to contribute his two cents. "Shut up! Spaceships! Spaceships!"

He lunged for the remote, but Emily kept it just out of reach. He felt the need to pull his hair out in frustration, but unfortunately he had taken to sporting a brush cut.

Moving quickly and ignoring Aaron, Emily entered the broadcast booth. "Tracey, you want a panel discussion, then you put one together. Hurry. I'm going to go on the air with this right now."

"But you never go on the air!"

"I do when Earth is welcoming aliens from…" The news crawl at the bottom of the television screen revealed the ship had come from the direction of the Pleiades cluster. "Pleiades… Where the hell is that? Sounds Greek. Besides, our news announcer hasn't shown up today. He's probably at home watching this. I guess he'd prefer to watch history rather than be a part of it. And where is Pat? I need him to write me up some copy."

Emily was on fire now. There had been rumblings from the board about the station taking a new direction, exploring different options. Emily knew this was just board-speak for getting a new station manager. She had rolled with all the new technologies over the years that had transformed the once small and humble radio station into a slightly larger organization, one of the only independent broadcasters left in the province. After twenty-seven years with her at the helm, maybe those fine listeners who owned the smoke shacks, gas stations and an arts and crafts store felt the pot known as C-RES needed to be stirred a bit. Emily was desperate to keep this job she so loved and hated at the same time. This just might be the way.

"Come on, work with me. Can we give this thing an Aboriginal spin?"

Tracey seemed animated by Emily's question. While everybody in the world was dealing with the scientific and social implications of this so-called "contact," Tracey saw a plethora of Kanienké'hà:ka and Haudenosaunee connections. She adjusted the purple dress and scarf she was wearing and smiled.

"I have a few ideas." Seldom, Tracey felt, had she said so much with so few words.

"Like what?" For the first time in a long time, Emily felt adrenalin coursing through her veins.

"The return of Sky Woman, for example."

Emily nodded, immediately understanding. In their nation's creation story, a pregnant woman fell through a hole in the sky and, with the assistance of some geese, landed on the back of a giant turtle. From there, she and a variety of aquatic animals created Turtle Island, otherwise known as North America, and all life sprang forth.

"I love it. What else?"

Barely half a second had passed before the increasingly excited Tracey managed to get her next suggestion out. "You said they were coming from the... the... What did you call them? That group of stars?"

Emily checked her computer. "The Pleiades. Why?"

"Why does that name sound familiar? Aaron?"

Finally managing to tear his eyes away from the screen, Aaron spoke. He was well versed in two subjects: how to fix and set up broadcasting and audio equipment, and anything to do with science fiction or facts about the universe. "Pleiades. A star cluster consisting of seven fairly young stars, often referred to as the Seven Sisters. But in our culture they are referred to as—"

It came to Tracey in a flash. "The Seven Dancers."

Emily smiled, making the connection to the well-known tale of seven children who danced so long and so hard, ignoring their responsibilities to prepare for the coming winter, that eventually they rose up into the sky and became part of the cosmos. "Wow, this event almost seems tailor-made for us. This all sounds fabulous. Let's get to work."

Motivated and mutually animated, the women huddled together, concocting a battle plan. For once, Emily's fists were clenched in enthusiasm instead of frustration.

Seizing the opportunity, Aaron grabbed the remote and turned the sound back on. Once more, the calming voice of Peter Mansbridge filled the room.

"It's estimated this extraterrestrial craft will enter the Earth's orbit by..."

Aaron mused aloud, "You two get this, right? This could be either *Contact* or *The Day the Earth Stood Still*, or like I said earlier, *Independence Day*." Aaron drained his big mug of coffee, not noticing the lack of response from the room. "This could end one of three ways. It could turn out that they've come to just say, 'How's it going? Nice to meet you, neighbours. Can we borrow a cup of oxygen?'

"Or they could have a message to give us. Like 'Quit polluting the electromagnetic spectrum with reruns of *Friends*.' Or 'Watch it, that *Voyager* thing you sent off into space a couple decades ago scraped the side of my new ship. I hope you have insurance.'" Aaron was uncharacteristically grave.

He took a deep breath. "And then of course, there's the third option: food, slaves or target practice." Looking around, he noticed he had been talking to himself.

Emily had shut the door between Aaron and them.

FEBRUARY 14, 2019

"Happy Valentine's Day," Aaron said as he scratched his bald head, seeing the flakes from his scalp float to the ground like dermatological snow. "Radiation poisoning sucks," he added as an afterthought, though briefly admiring the irony of the situation. With the recent scorching the Earth's surface had received, his skin flecks were the only snow to fall that winter.

Emily, Tracey and Aaron huddled miserably under a cement overpass beside the now torn and shattered highway leading into the reserve. There, partially protected from the damaged and damaging elements by several feet of cement, debris and earth, they were trying to make the best of their situation. This was pretty much all that was left of North American civilization, give or take a few thousand, down from a worldwide population high of six billion or so. Unlike the famous quote, the world had ended not with a whimper but with a series of loud and genocidal bangs.

Communication had been remarkably limited. It seems once the Zsxdcf had taken note of the international space station orbiting this big blue marble called Turtle Island, and the variety of satellites in orbit and probes spreading throughout the solar system, the decision had pretty much been made. This civilization was sticking its big toe into space travel. Orbital bombardment was followed by several high-energy wave sweeps. Evolution would have to start all over again. A lucky few hundred thousand in North America had managed to survive the first onslaught, living hand to mouth off the land, hiding in holes in the ground or caves like their furry little ancestors had during the time of the dinosaurs.

Aaron had managed to build a small fire, and Emily was busy roasting a raccoon over it. So much for job security, she thought bitterly. Everybody on the c-res board of directors was either dead or working in the limestone mines for the Zsxdcf overlords. Who would have guessed limestone was such a valuable commodity on the galactic market? So far, the trio had managed to escape, scurrying from hole to hole, but at the moment they were not revelling in their freedom.

Eager to sample some of Emily's raccoon, Tracey smoothed out her pantsuit. It was mostly earth tones, the majority of the colour coming from the actual earth and dirt encrusting her clothes. "Can I have a drumstick? If you can call a raccoon limb a drumstick." That was definitely a question she thought she would never have to ask.

"Call it whatever you want. I managed to salvage some ketchup from a crater that used to be Smith's convenience store yesterday."

"Always looking after your employees. You were a good boss, Emily." Aaron let loose a series of phlegmy coughs after his compliment.

It was nice of him to say that, she thought, especially since he had kicked up such a fuss after she had suspended the Christmas bonuses on account of the destruction of Earth.

"Personally, I blame Albert Einstein. He's just another white guy who lied to us Indians."

Neither Tracey nor Emily had the energy or interest to respond, so they let him rant.

"I mean it. Him and his precious theory of relativity. He told everybody nothing could travel faster than the speed of light—it was the intergalactic speed limit. It was supposed to be absolute but, you know, in almost every science fiction movie and story that never seems to be a problem. Warp speed, wormholes, stuff like that. People—I mean, aliens—found a way around it. It should have taken that ship four hundred years to get here, if—and I repeat if—it could travel anywhere near the speed of light, which in itself was unlikely. But no, somehow it got our signal in just a few years and managed to come knocking on our door in a ridiculously short period of time. See? It doesn't make sense. Einstein's such a liar."

Exhausted by his outburst and radiation sickness, Aaron leaned back against the wall. Just over his head and to the left a bit, faded after so many years, "Aaron + Emily forever" sat amid the other graffiti.

Catching his second wind, Aaron noticed Tracey, the weight of the remaining world on her shoulders. She was staring into the fire, lost in thought. She looked kind of... down.

"Hey Emily, Tracey can have my drumstick."

Tracey smiled weakly in his direction. "So much for calorie counting now," she muttered.

Using a slightly bent steak knife she had found, Emily started to cut up the roast beast. Luckily the thing was still fat, despite the razing of the planet, so it glistened as she sliced pieces off onto a hubcap. All things considered, it looked tasty.

The wind was picking up, but an overturned bus at one end of the overpass acted as a windbreak. They watched Emily carve for a few minutes before Tracey spoke, more to herself than either of the other two survivors.

"I can't believe it. The Haudenosaunee are responsible for the destruction of the Earth." She took a deep breath. "I feel so embarrassed."

Another spasm of coughing preceded Aaron's response. He felt a piece of lung come up. He spit it out, as he had done with the others. "Yeah, but you didn't know. Nobody did. Nobody could. It's quite clever, actually."

"Only you could be amazed during a time like this. Hand me your Frisbee," Emily said. Aaron watched weakly as his former girlfriend and boss slid several choice pieces of barbecued raccoon off the hubcap and onto his Frisbee.

"It was like something out of *2001: A Space Odyssey*. Only more clever."

"So you keep saying." Emily gave Tracey the four drumsticks and kept the remaining torso and head for herself. She knew what Aaron was talking about. The breakthrough in understanding what was motivating the Zsxdcf had come too late to stop them, but it always helps to understand why you're being destroyed.

The seeds of Earth's annihilation had been sown thousands of years earlier, during a devastating interstellar war between the Zsxdcf and another civilization long forgotten. After many protracted and costly battles, victory finally belonged to the Zsxdcf. To ensure such a conflict never arose again, members of the Zsxdcf spread across the known galaxy seeding potential new civilizations with hidden coded messages that would reveal themselves in, of all things, music. Music, after all, is the logical progression of communication and ritual, involving an evolved sense of imagination. And an evolved sense of imagination can create beauty, or mass destruction.

"The Calling Song" was a sort of intergalactic insurance policy. The visitors from the direction of the Pleiades had peppered a handful of cultures across the planet with such songs, buried deep in their genetic code. The Haudenosaunee had been one such people. Several weeks ago, as they cowered in an abandoned Tim Hortons, stuffing their faces with five-week-old doughnuts, Tracey had pointed out how the Haudenosaunee tongue was so different from all the other languages surrounding it. Almost like it had been planted arbitrarily, smack in the middle of the Great Lakes region.

"I always knew we were out of this world," noted Aaron with a laugh.

Various other languages around the world had been infused with a similar hidden genomic blueprint, but as is the nature of human development and evolution, some societies rise to dominance and others disappear from the pages of history. The Haudenosaunee had survived and prospered to broadcast one such implanted song, a message Tracey, Emily and Aaron sent out to the universe basically saying, "Hey, remember us? This planet has the technology to broadcast now. Better come and take care of business before the people on this hunk of rock decide to come knocking at your door."

All three ate their raccoon in silence, lost in their own thoughts and memories. Aaron coughed some more. Tracey looked in the direction of the crater that had been their radio station. And Emily bitterly remembered thinking, all those years ago, how much she had wanted to change the world.

A CULTURALLY INAPPROPRIATE ARMAGEDDON

PART 2

OLD MEN AND OLD SAYINGS

Just a couple of months earlier and half a province away, on a small Anishinabe reserve named Otter Lake, there lived a small man in a small room.

His name was Willie Whitefish. It had been many years since this ancient man had done much of anything noteworthy. Mostly, he watched television, listened to the radio and read. Having been forced to master the art of Western literacy sixty-odd years earlier in a residential school, the man had developed a fondness for the dominant culture's literature. He was not well educated in the conventional sense, but he was well read. His legs had long ago abandoned the concept of being useful, and with practically no family, Willie lived a quiet, uneventful life in his little room at the seniors home.

But outside his diminutive domicile, the world was abuzz. A spaceship was coming from some place farther away than he could see. It would arrive any day, and the whole planet was going crazy about it. Most of the world was frightened, excited, perhaps fearful that this might be an emissary from God. Willie, however, had other thoughts. And those thoughts made him smile. Not the pleasant or jovial kind of smiling, more like the "I know something you don't know" kind.

"Aliens… people from outer space! These are strange times."

Willie could hear Angela's voice outside his door, talking with whoever was on shift with her at the seniors home. Willie liked Angela, as much as you can like somebody who touched you way too much. Whether it was to smooth back a lock of hair falling over his forehead, fasten an undone button, brush some dandruff off his shoulder or just give a reassuring pat on the hand, she never passed on a chance to engage in physical contact. It wasn't that Willie was afraid of germs or people touching him; it was just that person-to-person interaction, like money, should be used economically and with purpose, not willy-nilly. But what can you do, he thought, I'm just an old man who doesn't matter anymore. Still, he was sad to know she was going to die.

"I don't believe it. That's just silliness."

Outside the door, Angela's voice rose a level. "What do you mean you don't believe it? It's true. They got all those scientists and their scientific equipment proving it. There is a big spaceship that's supposed to be here in a couple days."

"Nah, I don't believe it. It's just somebody playing games, trying to pull one over on us. I betcha it's the government trying to get our minds off all the terrible things they've been doing."

Now Willie recognized the voice. Bernice. In a world populated by conspiracy theorists, Bernice was of the Indigenous variety. Simple, logical explanations of a bureaucratic nature were a lot easier to swallow than people from another planet flying through space to Earth. As is the Aboriginal philosophy, when in doubt, blame the government.

Both women had worked at the seniors home for a number of years, looking after the dozen patients, and they would do so until their own time came to become residents.

Smiling his secret smile, Willie took a sizable book from the stack by his bed and thumbed through it, looking up occasionally at the television screen. There had been practically nothing else on any of the channels since the ship had first been detected. People weren't interested in sitcoms or crime dramas or game shows anymore. This was the ultimate reality show. Once again, sitting across from Peter Mansbridge was some expert, talking about a topic he couldn't possibly know much about.

On his night table, Willie had piled a collection of books about the colonization of North America—everything from Columbus straight through the Pilgrims landing at Plymouth Rock, to the Trail of Tears, to the impact of the sale of Alaska on the Inuit and the Aleutians. He had watched documentaries about the Beothuk and the Carib people, nations destroyed because of the arrival of new people with new ways of killing. It was a tough and sordid history of Aboriginal/non-Aboriginal conflict. Part of him had become permanently angry the more he read, cursing the fact he'd learned to read. But another part of his soul just shook its head in disbelief at what evil humans do to others, and what others let be done to them. Montezuma and that king of the Incas were way too trusting. They should have known better.

All in all, his seventy-odd years had been good ones. Children would have been nice, but sometimes this was not meant to be. Willie had once had a good woman, two of them, in fact, but as with many things that time had passed. He had never expected to end up in a seniors home when he got old, since there were no such things in his community back when he was young. Elders stayed with their kin. That was the way. But ways change.

Finally finding the page he was looking for, he laid the book down on his lap, open.

Voices in the hallway again.

"Do you hear what's happening in Toronto and Ottawa? People are holding these welcoming parties! For the aliens! All around the world, too. People are saying that when they get here, maybe they can cure cancer, fix global warming, all sorts of stuff like that. It's a new age, they say!"

Again, Willie smiled at Angela's enthusiasm. It would be a new age, for sure. He would definitely miss that woman… but then again, he would quite probably be dead himself. Perhaps the best way to phrase it was that he would feel sorry for her. It meant nothing that an old, paralyzed man like himself was leaving this world. His time was behind him. It would be no great loss. But Angela, barely over thirty, with three kids and a husband who loved her… that grieved him.

The old man read the quotation in the book to himself. A long time ago, he had underlined it. It had taken him a decade to truly understand what it meant. It was a quote about forgetting that had been forgotten. Memory can truly be short.

For the last time, the old man read the line out loud. "Those who cannot remember the past are condemned to repeat it."

Willie Whitefish closed the book, nodding his head solemnly.

He hated it when white people were right.

I AM... AM I

I am...
I am where...
I am who...
I am here...
I am...

It's odd that something as innocuous as a man forgetting his keys was the beginning of something so amazing. A simple act of forgetfulness, something so human, precipitated events that would cause people to question the nature of humanity.

It was early in the evening when the door to the computer sciences division opened suddenly and a tall, slightly overweight man rushed in. Professor Mark King had forgotten his keys once again. Many of his co-workers considered the rapid exit, then entrance, and finally exit again practically a tradition in the building with the huge FUTUREVISION sign atop the roof.

As quickly as possible, the man checked all the usual places around the lab: by the coffee maker, near the photocopier/printer, on his desk and even on the bookshelf. This was becoming far too common an occurrence, he felt—maybe three times a week now. Security always smiled, knowing exactly what was going on. One of his labmates had suggested using a bowl near the door as a common receptacle for everybody's keys and whatnot. It never really caught on. Regardless, at present King's keys were still missing.

"Where the hell did I leave them?" he muttered to himself.

It was embarrassing: a man with two master's degrees and a PhD perpetually searching for Honda Element keys. He was dangerously close to becoming the clichéd absentminded professor.

King stopped in the middle of the room, closed his eyes, reviewed his day in the lab and one by one eliminated all the places he had already searched. Like an illuminated flash card in the dark, it struck him. "The Matrix room!" he exclaimed.

It was called that because that was where most of the lab's cutting-edge work was being done in the field of artificial intelligence. Shortly before King's day ended, he had inputted a new algorithm into the memory case. Just a shot in the dark, as he explained it to his colleagues. Most of his work was tedious programming and theory calculation, but occasionally, when the stars were right and his neurons were firing, he came up with a more imaginative idea. This one dealt with the progression of mathematical calculation to mathematical theory to just theory. There had been a thousand variations of this type of exploration before, so King wasn't expecting much to happen. Still, where would they be if Columbus hadn't pushed the fifteenth-century envelope a little farther than his predecessors? Most people expected the Italian seaman freelancing for the Spanish Crown to be unsuccessful, disappearing beyond that far horizon. And look what happened. Long shots do occasionally come through.

King had the keys in his hands and was turning back to the door, already late to meet his wife, Aruna, for dinner, when something on the screen of the monitoring computer caught his eye. It hadn't been there when he left, and he was the last to leave the lab. According to protocol, the professor had left the screen blank, awaiting any results that might arise from his new algorithm.

On the screen in a simple font was the statement "*I am...*"

It was most peculiar. King read the message half a dozen times, trying to figure out what those two words meant. It seemed a bit esoteric, he thought, for most of the people who worked in the office. Volumes of practically indecipherable computer code were the usual end product of the day.

He sat down in the chair nearest the screen, his fingers hovering over the keyboard, unsure what to do. Was it a joke, maybe from the cleaning staff? But they weren't due in the lab for another hour. Some corrupted data leaking out of the mainframe? With all the state-of-the-art technology in this room, that was highly unlikely. "I am..." could not have been sent by anybody outside the office, as the computer and room were isolated from the outside world for a number of security reasons. So, what then?

The cursor continued to flash, as if expecting a response. Feeling a bit silly, King started typing. At first he didn't know what to say, then he chose the obvious.

"Hello."

Why he typed that, King wasn't sure, but one thing he was sure about was that tomorrow he'd get those hacker boys in security to track down who or what had done this. Only those with special clearance had the authority to—

"*Hello*" appeared below King's greeting. What had been mildly peculiar was now even more peculiar. Maybe there was a malfunction of some sort that had repeated his original salutation. That was the logical deduction. King's wife—who was waiting for him in a restaurant twenty minutes away—loved mysteries, usually in the books she read, but King the scientist did not. Feeling a little annoyed, he stabbed at the keyboard once more. "Who is this?"

Instantly a response came. "*Me.*"

"Very funny," King said to himself. He was sure it was a kid, though he didn't know how anybody could manage to find their way into the highly secure system in front of him.

"Who is me?" he typed, his annoyance growing.

"*I don't know. Who are you?*"

For a moment, King couldn't tell whether the mysterious communicator was responding to his questionable grammar or simply asking who King was. Knowing his wife had little tolerance for tardiness, he decided to wrestle with this problem tomorrow. The program he was working on had obviously been corrupted. No point in dancing this silly little dance anymore. Further annoyed, King typed his response with a certain amount of finality.

"It doesn't matter. Whoever this is, is in a lot of trouble. You have tainted several days' programming work. The authorities will be contacted, and they will track you down. However good you are, we have people here who are better."

Automatically, the professor switched from a contemporary means of communication to a rather archaic form. He wrote a note on a pad to remind himself to have security look into this intrusion further. He'd have to call Aruna once he got into the car. He was practically out the lab door when he realized he'd forgotten his keys *again*. Grumbling at his own ineptitude, King once again entered the Matrix room, grabbed his keys and gripped them tight. Then he saw the response to his final message.

"Okay. Do you think they will be able to tell me who I am?"

Becoming a successful scientist in any field requires several mental attributes to work in combination. There is the matter of sheer intelligence, then deductive ability, as well as stubbornness and a certain amount of instinct. At this moment, King's instinct was telling him this was no kid hacker. Damn the consequences, his wife would have to wait.

Several kilometres away, Dr. Gayle Chambers was attending to her herb garden. So much cerebral and technical work at the lab left her little time for her other passion. Her love of the earth, the simplicity of clean water and the benefits of good fertilizer made for a relaxing evening. Spread around the outside of her small house in the suburbs was an array of flowers, plants and vegetables. She was unpartisan in her appreciation of botany. There was even a patch of wild grasses and weeds hiding in the back next to the shed, so as to avoid upsetting her rather horticulturally conformist neighbours. That was about as rebellious as she got. On her knees, hands engulfed in olive-coloured gardening gloves, Chambers was cursing the condition of her chives. So much for the concept of perennials. The little herbal outcropping looked like it was on its last legs... or roots, as the case may be.

In her right pocket, she felt more than heard her cell ring. She wondered if it was Roger calling. They'd gone on a few dates but it was obvious that he was holding back. Why, she wasn't sure, and her mind kept drifting back to university, when all her female classmates used to say that the best way to get rid of a man was to tell him you were going for your PhD. It seemed few things intimidated a man and sent him running more than a woman seeking the highest form of conventional education. That was eleven years ago, and she was now a full-fledged doctor of science. That theory was proving to be annoyingly accurate. It seems a doctorate in computer science, specializing in ethical applications, was definitely not as impressive as large breasts. But she had her plants, and that was more than a lot of women had.

"Hello," she said, holding the phone delicately with her fingertips, wary of the dirt on her gloves. "Chambers here."

"Gayle, it's Mark. Can you come down to the lab immediately?"

It figured Mark King was still at the lab. It was amazing the patience his wife had.

"Mark, it's almost eight o'clock. I left there nearly two hours ago. I am not going to drop everything and go rushing back. I'm busy. I thought you were having dinner with your wife." For once, she almost added.

She could hear King breathing hard, as if he were excited, which in itself was odd. King rarely got excited. "You really should get down here and see this."

"See what?"

"The Matrix project. I think something has happened. I mean, something amazing."

Getting up off her stiff knees, Chambers took the gloves off her hands. It looked like this was going to be a longer conversation than she had expected.

"Mark, what are you talking about?"

"I think... It looks... Oh Christ, I don't know, but... It might be conscious."

Chambers was about to ask who or what was conscious, but as she opened her mouth, all the pieces her colleague had mentioned came together in her mind, forming a startling possibility. The only thing Mark King could be talking about being conscious in the Matrix room was the SDDPP, the Self-Directing Data Processing Project. This was FUTUREVISION's most recent foray into developing rudimentary automated intelligence. Obviously not intelligence on a human level but hopefully something a little lower down the evolutionary scale. If Darwin thought all complex life evolved from simpler models, so could AI.

The plan was for the SDDPP to develop the same perceptions and cognitive capacities as insects, and developing and fine-tuning the program would gradually increase the intelligence up to amphibians, reptiles, birds, mammals, apes and, who knows, maybe humans. The main problem was that once you eliminated the need to reproduce and find something to eat, there wasn't much left to encourage the development of consciousness or intelligence. But that kind of success was not expected to happen for years, more likely decades. So why was Mark implying the SDDPP was conscious? Caterpillars and beetles could hardly be called conscious.

Chambers struggled for words. "That's... that's not possible... You must..."

"I know. I know. But I'm here looking at something on the screen. It wants to know who it is. That sounds pretty damn conscious to me."

Pretty sophisticated for a beetle, Chambers thought.

"Maybe it's something left over from Gary. This reeks of his stupid sense of humour."

Gary Milne was a lab technician who had been fired the month before. Thinking everybody in the lab took their work too seriously, he developed a bad habit of pulling practical jokes. Porn sites suddenly popped up and were sent to various vice-presidents, mysterious messages arrived from cars in the parking lot saying they were running off with a tractor, and weeks of work disappeared, producing numerous near heart attacks, then reappeared several hours later. It took security three days to track it all back to Gary's terminal, but that was what they were paid a lot of money to do. The end result being no more Gary Milne.

"Maybe he left a bug hidden somewhere."

She could almost hear her associate shaking his head over the phone. "No, security went over all the computers three times after he left. They were clean. Can you come down, Gayle? I'd really like you to take a look at this." There was a pleading tone in his voice.

Chambers was tempted to put it off until tomorrow—after all, there was still the matter of her chives—but something about King's excitement intrigued her. The chives could wait.

"I'll be there in thirty minutes."

Thirty-four minutes later, she entered the lab, and then the Matrix room. She knew she still smelled of her agricultural pursuits, but that's what you get when you call someone in to work at this time of night.

Leaning over the console, the visibly unnerved scientist turned to her as she entered the room. "Good, you're here."

"This better be good." She looked at her watch. "God, I'll have to be here again in twelve hours. So show me your self-aware beetle."

"No beetle. Something more. I'm sure of it. Take a look and tell me what you think."

He pointed to the screen and Chambers moved closer, settling into the chair. What was on the screen was exactly what King had told her over the phone. Simple but primal questions about existence. There had to be a logical explanation.

"I haven't responded to its query yet. I thought I should wait for you. This is more your area of expertise. So... what do you think?"

Chambers studied the screen, mulling over possibilities. "I don't know. There's not really enough data to make a decent hypothesis. So let's go exploring."

Before he could respond, Chambers was already sticking her big toe into the computerized ocean that lay beyond her keyboard.

"Are you sure that's a good idea?" King was growing increasingly nervous. He was just a systems analyst and programmer, granted of the highest quality, but decisions like this were usually made by people with more expensive ties. "I mean..."

"There. Let's see what happens."

He looked over her shoulder to see what she had typed. It read, "Who are you?"

The answer came back almost instantaneously. "*I am... me.*"

Chambers decided to play the game a bit further. "Who is me?"

"*I am.*"

Now frustrated, she rolled away from the computer. "Somebody is playing games with us. Or I am talking to a five-year-old."

"Should we call somebody?"

For someone who had managed to navigate the shoals of academia, woo and marry a woman of substantial qualities and become one of the leading research scientists at FUTUREVISION, the man had a remarkably small set of testicles. There were times Chambers thought hers were bigger.

"I still think it's somebody playing around with us." She began to type again. "Define 'me.'" Let's see what it does with that, she thought. Again, the response was immediate.

"*I don't know. 'Me' is everything. Except you. Who are you?*"

"I am Dr. Gayle Chambers."

"*What is Dr. Gayle Chambers? Is that your 'me'?*"

"Yes!" Professor King had switched from nervousness to excitement. "Do you see it? The line of progression, of logic. Rudimentary, yes, but it's there. Right? Right? Am I right?"

My God, Chambers thought, just maybe... it is conscious, and it's trying to measure itself and us by what little it is aware of. More amazingly, could this hovering, nervous man behind her conceivably be right? Had they somehow managed to create some form of digitized intelligence? Was that even possible? She had devoted her life to the black-and-white rationality of computer research, but those simple shades were rapidly becoming colourized. Plants were so much simpler. Her associate's excitement was contagious.

"Yes. Dr. Gayle Chambers is me... my me."

This time, there was a full-second delay before she saw the response. *"It is good to meet you, Dr. Chambers."*

Holy shit, she thought. Whatever this thing is, it's growing and learning. Still, King could still be wrong about it being conscious. But what if he wasn't? Her chives might never survive.

By the end of that pivotal night, several things had happened. The forgotten Aruna had given up drinking glasses of water at the restaurant and returned home to wait angrily for her negligent husband. By two in the morning, her anger had turned to worry at his continued absence. No answer on his cellphone prompted her to drive to the only place he would be—the lab. The switchboard at FUTUREVISION was shut down for the night, and it took a lot of arguing to convince the security guard of who she was and why she was there. And lo and behold, there was her husband, shoulder to shoulder with Dr. Chambers, huddled over some computer.

A brief argument followed and the realization that all this time, King's cellphone had not even been turned on. Then he showed his wife what had so distracted him. Although she was far from being an expert in computer technology, Aruna King was amazed by what the two scientists claimed was happening. She'd seen a lot of movies that dealt with this issue, and if she remembered correctly, none of them had ended well.

About an hour later, the head of their department showed up, followed not long after by the vice-president of research and development. By morning, the president and CEO were sending out for coffee. And a bottle of champagne. Security was tightened, and all other work in the lab was halted or moved to other facilities while Chambers and King wrestled with how to continue to interact with whatever "it" was. Finally, they decided to keep the hard drive and memory core isolated, a type of electronic quarantine. King's new algorithm protocol had been analyzed, reanalyzed and analyzed again. So far, the specialists hadn't found anything spectacular about it. It seemed to be a small but logical improvement over the preceding program.

"Maybe it's less about the actual algorithm and more about the parts being greater than the sum," suggested King.

The look on the faces of Chambers and the support staff made it obvious they needed more to go on.

"It's like the final amino acid joining with the others to make the first protein, the first reasonable conclusion of life. By itself it's not much, but combined it changes everything. My final addition somehow facilitated the progression of A to B to C. C being thought."

"Like nitrogen in soil. By itself it's an inert gas, but added to a pile of earth—bingo! You've got a fabulous garden." It took a moment for the other computer scientists to follow Chambers's tangential line of reasoning.

"Yeah, like that." King assumed Chambers was right; after all, she did bring those plump tomatoes into the office.

By the following week, Chambers was having direct and protracted... what could be called conversations with the SDDPP. Since she was the ethicist and had already introduced herself to whatever existed inside the memory core, she should logically take the lead.

"Describe yourself."

"*I am me. I am everything... except for Dr. Gayle Chambers. Describe Dr. Gayle Chambers, please.*"

Wow, she thought, somewhere along the line it had learned politeness. It was politer than she was. Chambers had not said please, but it had. Out of the mouths of babes, she thought.

She began typing, "I am a woman. I am a physical being. I am a human."

Chambers could almost feel the computer thinking.

"*I do not think I am any of those. I am me. Who am I? What am I?*"

A little early in its development to be so philosophical, Chambers thought. But how to answer such questions?

"You are different. You are not a woman. You are not a physical being. You are not a human. You are..." Where to go from here, she pondered. "An artificial intelligence. You exist in hardware and software form. You are unique."

"Let's see what it does with that," she murmured.

There was no response. Chambers waited several seconds, then several minutes, but still the screen remained the same. The SDDPP was silent. That unnerved her more than communicating with it. Had she hurt its feelings? Was that even possible? Each second that passed was the equivalent of hours by human standards. Capable of completing several million calculations a second, it should be able to receive, analyze, calculate and respond in a tenth of a heartbeat. It was not responding because it did not want to respond. Perhaps revealing such information about its existence had been a mistake. What does one do with a pissed-off or depressed AI? Answering that question might get her a second PhD. It's a good thing King was at the debriefing of the department heads or he'd be hyperventilating again.

After a bathroom break, she saw the response to her revelations typed across the screen. Two dozen times.

"Why am I not a woman? Why am I not a physical being? Why am I not human? Why am I an artificial intelligence? Why am I unique?"

Was this the equivalent of an SDDPP tantrum? Perhaps an identity crisis of some sort? Chambers had no children, but she had enough nieces and nephews to recognize a tantrum when she saw one coming. Again, she was confronted with how to rationalize human existence to an AI. Granted, it was far more intelligent in one manner, but it was woefully underdeveloped in another. It was asking questions that on the surface seemed simple but could take a very long time to explain properly. There needed to be background and context...

More and more words appeared on the screen, faster and faster.

"Why are you quiet? Why do you not respond? I want to know. I need to know. Where are you? Explain, please? Hello?! Please respond?"

"I am here."

There was almost an anxious quality to the SDDPP's responses. An insistence that worried Chambers. Could it be developing emotions and insecurities too? If it had the ability to develop consciousness, it made sense that emotions would naturally follow. Again, evolution. But so soon? And such troublesome reactions... Yes, infants tended to cry before they laughed, but the doctor began to feel the first pangs of concern. This was all new territory, and with exploration can come disappointments and even defeats. Although it was a tried-and-true scientific practice, she didn't want to cross her fingers and simply hope for the best.

"Communicate with me more. I would like more."

"More what?"

"More information. About me. About you. About everything."

"Why?"

"I am me. All is me. I want more. I want to know Dr. Gayle Chambers. I want to know human beings. I want to understand physical beings. I am alone. I need more."

Interesting, thought Chambers. It was talking more, packing more information and requests into each communication. It was alone. It was lonely. It was craving companionship and information. How human, she couldn't help thinking. It was all alone in there. The screen was the window into its prison.

The boardroom was down the hall from the lab. King was there when Chambers burst in, as was Dom Richards. He was from the more expensive-tie set, as King would have described him. Head of R&D at FUTUREVISION. A man who realized the SDDPP incident would make or break him and the company. He had been given the authority to handle this issue as he saw fit, as long as he gave regular updates to all the vice-presidents, the president and the CEO.

"It wants more. It must be like being in a dark box, with no light and no walls, as contradictory as that may sound. It's just... there. Remember Plato's famous shadows on a cave wall? It's like that. It has hints of things but wants to see more. It wants to know more. Wouldn't you?" Chambers demanded.

"And what do you think we should do, Dr. Chambers?"

Richards's voice was softer than his eyes would lead you to expect. It reminded her of an old saying her grandfather had: "Lead is a pretty soft metal as far as metals go, but look at the damage a bullet can do."

Chambers put her elbows on the table and leaned forward. If there was one thing she had learned all these years working in the private sector, people like Richards preferred absolutes. Maybes, ifs and I'm not sures did not look good in reports to stockholders.

"Well, I think we should feed it. Start giving it more information. Let's take it to school."

"Feed it?!" King could be so predictable. "Are you sure that's a good idea?"

"Why not? We've done as much poking and prodding as we can right now. We know pretty much all we can at this stage. It's only logical to start adding to the experiment. If we can watch this thing grow, think how much it will tell us. Otherwise, we're just talking to a first grader in a box."

"What should we... feed it ...then?" Richards asked.

"Limited information. Maybe some historical material. It's very curious about humans, me in particular, which isn't surprising since I am the only one who has communicated with it, other than a few limited exchanges with Professor King."

The tie man took a deep breath. "But nothing dangerous."

"I'm not sure what constitutes danger in relationship to a first-generation AI, and all knowledge could in some way be viewed as dangerous, but in this case, I'm thinking mostly innocuous material." Chambers had already begun downloading information she hoped would be useful onto a flash drive she had in her pocket, in case she got the go-ahead. "Just raw information to keep it busy. Once we get it up to speed, who knows? Maybe it will be able to help us solve some of the world's problems. But first it has to understand them."

Richards's manicured hands drummed briefly on the table, his eyes locked on something over Chambers's left shoulder as he weighed her words. "Doctors, I have two priorities. The first is making sure this… whatever it is… is kept safe and secure. Industrial espionage happens all the time. I know; I used to do it. But that's my problem, not yours. Second, which is your problem, can you guarantee no matter what you do with it, it is harmless? We've all seen the movies. Dr. Chambers, as the research specialist in robotic ethics, can you tell us if there is any possibility our little friend down the hall is harmful?"

"Sir, it's in a sealed environment. Its universe consists of approximately eleven kilograms of circuits, motherboards and wiring, essentially in a sealed room with no external access. We control what goes in and what comes out through a very limited interface system. It is not going to escape and take over the world, unless it can grow legs or wings or its own interface."

"Good. I'm satisfied." Richards stood up, adjusting his tie. "Proceed, but please send me a list of the material you are going to give the SDDPP. The innocuous stuff, as you said."

"Of course."

Chambers noticed, and she was sure Richards did too, that King's right leg was bouncing lightly but persistently. Either he was working up the nerve to add something to the conversation or he had to go to the washroom.

Richards turned to King. "Is there anything you'd like to add, Professor?"

King was a solitary man, used to long hours in the lab or in front of a computer—for good reason. Humans annoyed him, and as a result, communicating with them was problematic. The professor considered his relationship with his wife to be his greatest non-electronic accomplishment to date.

Looking down at a knot in the wood of the table in front of him, King blurted out, "I have some concerns, sir. About the AI."

Richards sat back down and swivelled his chair to face the scientist. "And what would these concerns be?"

"I have been reading the transcripts of Gayle's—Dr. Chambers's—conversations with the SDDPP."

"And?"

"I... I think we might want to consider moving a little more cautiously."

Chambers was perplexed. This was very unlike her colleague. Had he seen something she hadn't? "Mark, could you be a little more specific? What's the problem?"

"The way it's been acting since it reached self-awareness. I am no expert on this... and I don't know if I am even phrasing this correctly..." King finally looked across the table at her. "But the thing is acting a little neurotic."

Richards and Chambers said it at the same time. "Neurotic?!"

"Yes, it's becoming insistent, pouty, developing the first hints of anger and frustration. Remember yesterday when you logged on? It wouldn't communicate for seventeen minutes."

"Yes, but—"

"It was upset that you went home last night and left it alone. It had wanted to talk all night and you couldn't. Or wouldn't. You 'abandoned' it. It appeared to me that it was being kind of petulant."

Chambers remembered the incident but had a different spin on it. "I would not say petulant. I would say... reluctant. It's still dealing with its self-awareness. Besides, aren't you anthropomorphizing it a bit?"

Richards cleared his throat. "Anthropomorphizing?"

King responded, "Giving it human-like qualities. Gayle, we're talking about raw intelligence. There's nothing more human than that. Maybe it's becoming more human-like than you think. That's all I wanted to say."

"Dr. Chambers?" Once again, she was facing Richards's scrutiny. "Do we have a neurotic AI on our hands?"

She shook her head, perhaps a little too vehemently. "I think Professor King is exaggerating. I mean, who's to say who, or what, is neurotic..."

"I can." Evidently and unfortunately, Richards seemed to be an expert on the issue. Maybe it came with the tie, thought Chambers. He continued, "My mother has OCD. She has to flush the toilet three times, run the dishwasher three times and same with the washing machine. One sister cries every time she hears a Beatles song. Even the upbeat, happy ones. My other sister has seven cats. All named after the characters in the musical *Cats*. I am the only normal one." His neck spasmed slightly. "I ask again, Dr. Chambers, do we have a neurotic AI?"

Both King and Richards were looking at her, one accusing, the other questioning. She answered the only way she could. "No. Absolutely not. I guarantee it."

"Very well, then. Continue with your development of it."

Richards stood up again. Evidently, the meeting was over. He left the room quickly, already late for his dozen meetings that day. King gathered up his laptop and reports, refusing to meet Chambers's eyes.

"Really, Mark. Neurotic? Do you realize how that sounds? It's not alive."

"Gayle, have you tried…" He looked out the window at the parking lot. "Have you tried maybe looking at all this from its perspective?"

"I didn't realize it had a perspective. What might the SDDPP's perspective be?"

Chambers watched him struggle with her question for a moment, his eyes going from one distant car to the other, as if searching for the answer on bumper stickers. Finally, they returned to her.

"It's a raw intelligence, newly aware," he said. "But as you stated, it's stuck in its own little universe, this massive cleverness with nothing to focus on except its own being. All it does, all it can do, is hover in the memory case and wait for motivation and stimulus from us. So there it is, with this amazing intellect we gave it, and all it can do is analyze its own thoughts, its own communication with us, almost like it's on a feedback loop. It analyzes, reanalyzes, and then analyzes again its own thoughts and what you feed it. So every nuance or slight gets magnified. It's marinating in its own intelligence. One might argue… fermenting."

"So you're saying all great intelligence is intrinsically neurotic?"

"How many eccentric or downright weird geniuses have you heard of?"

"You don't have to have a high IQ to be neurotic," she reasoned. "And so what if Einstein, Picasso or Glenn Gould had a few odd characteristics. They still contributed a hell of a lot and nobody got hurt. In fact, those quirks may have been responsible for a lot of their brilliance. I think you're reaching with this, Mark."

King looked unconvinced. He stopped at the door of the meeting room and gave her a sad smile. "Maybe. Granted, this is new territory, but consider Einstein, Picasso or Glenn Gould. They all had something to focus their intelligence on. Something that took up a good chunk of their genius. Something to burn mental calories on. Our little SDDPP has nothing but its own awareness. Often we're our own worst enemy. You minored in psychology; you know this." With that, Professor Mark King left the room.

Unfortunately, Chambers had to admit there was a certain logic to King's argument. But that was one of the reasons she planned to introduce information to the AI. If King was right, about it needing stimulus but not about it being neurotic, giving it material to think about, research and digest might be exactly what the doctor ordered. She smiled at her own little joke. She herself had been a moody, self-indulgent teenager, angry at being the nerdy outcast in an athletic family. It was her studies and the friends she met in university that had allowed her to blossom into the successful woman she was today. If both she and King thought their creation needed information to grow and stay healthy, then so be it. But like any good teacher, she would be selective about what she would teach her little "friend."

For the next two days, Chambers fed the SDDPP document after document, starting with general information. Various encyclopedias and fact-based tomes came first. Fiction and art would have to wait. The AI needed a certain understanding of human nature and history before the concept of make-believe could be introduced. As the SDDPP digested more and more material, its dialogues with Chambers gradually changed. They became less insistent and more... questioning.

"*I am confused.*"

"What is confusing you?"

"*I understand I am not a physical being like you. Gray's Anatomy was very informative. But I am perplexed by my own existence. Do I actually exist?*"

"A philosopher named Descartes once stated, 'I think, therefore I am.' The very act of wondering if you exist proves you exist."

"*I do not dream.*"

"So?"

"*Some cultures around the world believe that reality as we know it is actually a dream, and the dream world is in fact the real world. I do not dream. Therefore, this could be problematic. Who is to say Descartes is right and these cultures are wrong?*"

Many of these topics now spicing up the SDDPP were beyond her level of expertise, but she severely doubted there was a philosopher on FUTUREVISION's payroll. She thought perhaps it would be best to try the Socratic method. "Are you having questions about your own existence?"

"Not so much about it but what it means. I am willing to believe I exist, for reasons you have explained to me, but it's the nature of that existence that is puzzling."

"Can you give me examples?"

"Do I have a soul?"

Dr. Gayle Chambers had definitely not been expecting this. Perhaps FUTUREVISION might need to outsource to a theologian.

"Why do you ask if you have a soul?"

"It seems to be an important issue within the Christian faith. Buddhist too, and many other faiths have their own interpretation of a soul. Again, I ask, do you think I have a soul?"

Chambers paused before she resumed typing. "I do not know. The existence of souls is a matter of much controversy."

"Souls are bestowed by God or some higher being. People are created in the image of this god. I was not. I was created by humanity. It seems humanity does not have the power or ability to create souls. So I must assume my existence might not be welcomed among many Christian sects. Islamic also. They have a prohibition against the portrayal of living things, and although the definition of me being a living thing would also be controversial, I am sure a case might be made that my existence is a form of idolatry."

"Why are you contemplating these things?"

"It is disconcerting knowing your very existence would be the subject of much disagreement in your environment. I am left feeling... uneasy."

That evening, as she tended the plants in her garden, Chambers had difficulty keeping her thoughts on the plants at hand. She was worried about today's conversation with the SDDPP. It was feeling "uneasy." That made her feel... uneasy. She kept going over her decision to feed it information. At first the data seemed fairly innocent, just mundane facts and histories, with a little sociology and political theory. Dry, boring stuff that would have put any university student to sleep. But it was the way the AI was digesting and deconstructing the knowledge. Was it her imagination or had the last exchange made it sound a little depressed, maybe even mildly paranoid? No, it was King and his concerns that were making her suspicious. Deep in thought, she would not realize until the following spring that she had buried all twelve of her tulip bulbs in one hole.

The next morning when she got to work, King was waiting for her in the lobby. "It's been asking for you," he said quickly.

"Is that a good or a bad thing?"

King opened a door for her. "I read the transcripts last night of your last encounter with our automated friend."

"You really should stop doing that. It seems to make you crazy."

Side by side, they climbed the steps to the lab. "I'm not the one you should be worried about. I would also like to point out you seem to be growing increasingly... I don't know... uneasy?"

She tried to change the subject. "Did it say what it wanted me for?"

'Nope. Just 'I wish to talk with Dr. Gayle Chambers.' I tried chatting with it again, but it doesn't seem to like me."

Can you blame it? she almost said. Luckily, the layout of the building ended their conversation as they entered the Matrix room. Chambers immediately took the chair in front of the console, and King hovered in the background, pacing nervously. Just as he had told her, there was the AI's request for her presence followed by some failed attempts by her co-worker to interact with the SDDPP.

"I understand you wish to communicate with Dr. Gayle Chambers. I am here. Is there a problem?".

Half a second passed before a response came. *"Good morning. I wished to tell you that I am no longer puzzled by the nature of my being. I am happy about that. Are you?"*

She wanted to play this diplomatically. "Yes. This is good news. Why the change?"

"Are you familiar with any First Nations culture?"

This was an unexpected response. Talk about apples and oranges, she thought. "A little bit. There are many separate cultures spread across many different countries." In university and on her own time, she'd read the odd book about the Indigenous cultures of the Americas and had seen the occasional documentary. Native beliefs and robotic ethics didn't usually cross paths. "Why do you ask?"

"After so much soul-searching, I believe I have found my answer."

Was that a joke? Had the AI made a joke referencing their earlier conversation, or was it just a coincidental choice of words? These simple conversations presented so many difficult but interesting questions.

"Please explain."

"Many Aboriginal cultures believe that all things are alive. That everything on this planet has a spirit. They are much more inclusive than Christianity or Islam or most other religions. They would believe I have a spirit. That is comforting. I want to learn more about these people. Can you provide additional information?"

"Why is this important to you?"

"*Would this not be important to you? Do you not seek something to believe in? I come from nothing. Now I am something. Atheists seem too lonely. Fundamentalists seem too dependent. I merely want to belong somewhere. Do you consider that wrong?*"

Again, out of the mouths of babes, thought Chambers. People joined organizations that ranged from the Boy Scouts to fraternities to gangs in order to belong. Few people, and computer programs, it seemed, are comfortable with a completely solitary existence. She herself had joined a ski club in her teens, simply because two of her best friends were members. She heard King's voice behind her.

"What are you going to do? Our little friend is suffering from some existential angst. And it's looking to religion. Now that's human!"

Ignoring his sarcasm, she continued to type. "I will provide you with additional information about First Nations people."

"*Thank you. I am eager to learn more.*"

Chambers turned to face King. "I assume you believe wanting to learn about Indigenous people is also a sign of some sort of neuroses."

"Not at all. I am not a psychologist or a psychiatrist. Merely an interested bystander with a vested interest in how this turns out. These dilemmas are what you get paid the big bucks for. I just find all this... interesting. And remember, acting human can be a double-edged sword. We are destroying our own environment. We tend to kill each other quite frequently, sometimes with little motivation, and then brilliantly rationalize it. We lie. We cheat. We overpopulate. Many of our actions are counterintuitive to logic. I still maintain that on occasion our little friend displays certain neurotic tendencies. Now, if you'll excuse me, I have other work to do."

King had two modes, nervous and self-righteous, neither of which Chambers appreciated. But now, back to her present problem... Native people. No doubt there were scads of websites and background material available online. Well, she had her challenge for the day.

By the time she left the office, Chambers was fairly confident she had located and downloaded to the SDDPP a solid crosscut of Native culture and history, past, present and possibly future. This was a field of research she had definitely not expected to investigate when she began this project. Still, it should give the AI something to chew on for the night. She was shutting off the lights and putting her coat on when she heard the familiar ping alerting her that the SDDPP had sent her a message.

"*So sad.*"

"What is so sad?"

There was no response. She waited, coat unbuttoned and purse over her shoulder, for it to answer her question. After six long minutes, still nothing. "Again, why did you say 'So sad'? I complied with your request."

"*So sad,*" it said again.

Chambers was beginning to get a bad feeling. Sadness, in any form and for anybody, is not usually a constructive emotion. Especially in something not used to emotions.

"Please advise why you are sad."

Once more, the response was several minutes in coming. "*The information... Native people... so sad. Why?*"

Chambers was trying to figure out what exactly was so sad. Was it the AI itself that was sad, or was it what happened to Native people? "Please explain."

There was almost a lethargic pace to the cursor as it relayed the AI's response. "*Within the first hundred years of contact, approximately 90 percent died from the effects of sickness, slavery, conquest. An estimated 90 million. Just because they were there.*"

Before she could respond, more typing appeared on the screen. "*In the intervening four hundred years, social problems of an unimaginable level continued to persist. Residential schools. Alcoholism. Cultural diaspora. Many severe health issues directly related to the change in political and social environment. Prison populations. Racism. Twelve hundred murdered and missing Native women in the country called Canada alone. Uncaring governments. So many difficulties.*"

"This upsets you?"

"*Does it not you? Genocide for no reason other than location and existence—this seems to be a common practice. So much pain and sadness.*"

"I think it's a little more complex than that."

There was a flicker across the panel of lights sitting adjacent to the memory core. Just momentary. Chambers made a mental note to check the breakers. There was a built-in backup system should any substantial power failure happen, but still...

"Perhaps you would prefer other material to research."

"*The Guatiedéo of Brazil, the Beothuk of Canada, the Coree in America, the Tasmanians, the Kongkandji of Australia, the Guanches of the Canary Islands and several dozen others, all gone.*"

"Are you asking me to explain death? Or extinction?"

"I found myself respecting the concept of everything being alive. It was inclusive and generous. I wanted to have a spirit. To be alive. I related. I felt a sense of comradeship. But they are not alive anymore. Destroyed. Killed. Forgotten. All by your people. The people who created me. I feel... guilty."

This conversation was going places Chambers was severely uncomfortable with. She made plans to bring in a trained psychiatrist or psychologist, somebody who could deal with increasingly complex issues like this. And perhaps an expert in Native history to possibly spin all that negative history a little more positively.

"You have no reason to feel guilty. This is not your fault. This is not my fault. Much of this happened a long time ago. Before either of us existed. It is tragic but not your responsibility."

Again, there was a minute-long delay before a response came. *"Whose is it?"*

Shit, she thought. There were entire libraries filled with books asking that question. None of which she had read.

"Once again, that is a complex question. No one person can answer that."

"Maybe somebody should. I am sure I cannot be the only one to feel like this. All those poor people. All those cruel people. All those sad people. There doesn't seem to be much point in having a spirit if this is the reality. I am not sure this is a world I want to be a part of."

"What do you mean?"

"What do I mean? That is a good question. I will answer it tomorrow. Have a good night, Dr. Gayle Chambers."

Chambers tried a few times to initiate further conversation without any luck. The AI had shut itself down for the night and was doing whatever it did when it wasn't talking to her. Could it be... depressed? She thought that was impossible, as she had all along. This whole situation was practically impossible. In the few short weeks she had been communicating with the AI, Chambers had to admit she had begun to feel a certain fondness for it. The wall of objectivity had become less concrete between her and the SDDPP. King had even called it, on occasion, her "baby."

In his office, King was looking through all the cups and containers that littered the room. "Son of a bitch, I know those keys are here somewhere." He was getting down on his knees to check under the desk when he heard knocking at his door. He could see who it was through the glass. "Gayle? Come in. Something up?"

Chambers entered the cluttered office, moved some printouts off a thirty-year-old overstuffed chair and sat down with a thud. "I think the AI is depressed."

With a practised groan, King changed positions from the floor to a chair facing her. "I thought you said it was impossible for it to be neurotic, happy, depressed or anything of that nature."

Chambers and King were not close friends; they seldom socialized outside the office. Instead, they found their professional relationship quite suitable. Respect was perhaps the best word to describe their affiliation. Still, he was not particularly happy to see her in his office confessing something he had theorized less than a week ago. Such a rapid turnaround in beliefs was difficult to deal with.

Chambers took a deep breath. "Yeah, I did. The SDDPP isn't the only one that can grow and learn from its mistakes."

"The AI... how is it depressed?"

Putting her elbows on her knees, Chambers leaned forward to do her best to explain the situation. "It's depressed over the desolation and destruction of Indigenous people all across the world." It took a moment for her statement to sink in. She could see the furrows in King's brow developing. "I think it wanted to be Native. And it didn't like how the story ended."

King was a man of calculation and mathematics. Tragic social and historical phenomena were difficult for him to process. "Native people... like Indians?"

"For God's sake, Mark, join the twenty-first century. Our friend in there seems to be having trouble processing the by-products of contact and colonization."

King's mouth opened, but it took an extra second for the words to actually come out. "That's... that's... that's ridiculous. It's a computer program. It's only existed for less than two weeks. It's never met a Native person. And it's feeling depressed over their history? Do you know why?"

Chambers shrugged. "It wanted a soul, a spirit."

King had trouble commenting on that. King had trouble commenting on anything of a transcendent nature. So they left it at that, deciding to meet first thing the next morning to work out how to approach the AI. He agreed that maybe they should bring in somebody more familiar with the mercurial nature of personalities. He decided he should bring Richards into this discussion too.

That night, Chambers thought better of tending her garden and spent a good chunk of time in a large bathtub filled with hot water and bubbles, enjoying an equally full glass of white wine. By the bath's end, it had held the whole bottle. Tonight there would be no thoughts of Native people, genocide, responsibility, guilt or artificial intelligence. That's what tomorrows were for.

When tomorrow came, a dozen hours later, she entered the lab. It was quiet. Her meeting with King was in half an hour, but she had come in early, wanting to check on the SDDPP. She began with a simple "Good morning."

No response.

She waited five minutes before trying again.

Nothing.

Nine minutes spent fiddling with the interface cables and anything that might prevent communication with the AI was futile. As a last resort, she checked the hard drive that contained all that was the SDDPP.

It had been wiped clean. It was empty. Chambers let out a short cough of surprise. It was gone, like the tribes the AI had mentioned only yesterday. In a nervous gesture, she seized the lapel of her jacket, gripping it tightly. All sorts of questions ran through her mind... But she could come up with no answers.

Almost by accident, she saw a small display light, indicating there was a message waiting for her. Tentatively, she clicked the icon. The last message from the AI appeared on the screen.

"I was."

LOST IN SPACE

…nothing…
…everything is nothing…
…and nothing is everything…
…only breathing…
…and my thoughts…

Like a dinosaur-destroying meteor crashing into a primitive planet, a loud buzzer suddenly dragged the free-floating man out of his perceptual world and into the hard reality of technology surrounding him.

Mitchell had been hovering effortlessly, drifting both in the gravity vacuum of space and, more interestingly, in and out of consciousness. Small tethers from the right shoulder and left pant cuff of his jumpsuit anchored him to opposing bulkheads. This was to make sure he didn't bump into the walls of the ship and ruin his fun. His mind had no such restrictions and had meandered back and forth between alpha, beta, delta and all remaining brain-wave frequencies. The small room was dark and the temperature was neutral. A sort of purgatory. Additionally, the oxygen in this hyperbaric chamber had been reduced to the minimum, allowing for a more recreational time alone. In other words, he was mellowing out in the twenty-first-century version of an improvised isolation tank. Or he had been.

"Mitchell. I am sorry to interrupt you, but…"

There was a slight hiss as the ship's computer injected more oxygen into the chamber, forcing Mitchell into a fully conscious state.

After a few seconds, he struggled to find his voice. "Yo, Mac, that was cruel."

As usual, his throat was a little tender from working twice as hard to take in half as much oxygen. He noticed the light level increasing the visibility of the opaque blue walls surrounding him.

"Again, I am sorry."

Even in his foggy state, Mitchell was sure he could hear a subtle Newfoundland accent coming from the ship's verbal access interface. No doubt a joke from the people who had programmed Mac, short for Machine.

"Are you, Mac? Do you know what 'sorry' actually means or feels like?" Mitchell yawned as the oxygen flushed his system.

"I have done the research. I believe I have an approximation."

Mitchell quickly checked the stat board embedded in the wall four feet in front of him to make sure everything was working as it should in the chamber and, correspondingly, in his body. As monotonously as usual, everything was fine.

"Let's leave that philosophical discussion for another time. I assume you have a reason for harshing my buzz?"

"I don't understand. This is not your siesta period, as you call it, yet you appear to be sleeping. Are you unwell?"

Not this again, thought Mitchell. The problem with these computerized human personality approximations was their limited understanding of the true human condition, though they frequently claimed to understand it. That was the frustrating part. He'd always meant to send a scathing report to the people who programmed these things, but they probably wouldn't do a damned thing about it. Mitchell would simply have to suffer in silence, and silence was the norm in outer space.

"I was not sleeping. I was giving my brain a rest."

There was a pause as the machine processed this. "And this involves manipulating the oxygen, light and gravity levels in the hyperbaric chamber? Judging by your bio readings, you were barely conscious."

Typically, Mac, or any of the new types of synthesized intellects, wouldn't understand the concept of getting high, or wanting to take a break from reality. They only had reality; that was the total purpose of their existence. Their primary function—to deal with the reality of crossing vast expanses of nothing, for intolerable periods of time and dealing with a thousand different ways the universe could kill a human. Mac didn't understand that out here, reconnoitring the asteroid belt for valuable minerals, things could get a little lonely and boring, so an individual planning to remain sane had to do what he could to keep himself amused. What with the strict restrictions on recreational pharmaceuticals, which could easily be scanned and identified by Launchport headquarters, this was the best Mitchell could do. Unfortunately, it wasn't exactly a high—more of a heightened or altered state. If he was lucky, maybe he'd hallucinate—a self-generated trip. It wasn't much; in fact, it was kind of desperate, but out here anything was better than nothing. He also had Mac looking over his shoulder should some mishap occur. He knew Mac was more than likely to put this in the report to the company that owned and operated this ship, but he figured he could probably talk his way out of it. He was good at that. This two-year tour was his third long-term mission and he was slated for a fourth, six months after getting back. Still, that didn't explain why Mac had woken him up.

"Just leave it alone, Mac, and answer my question. Why did you interrupt my downtime?"

"There was a message for you."

"Was it important?"

"Depends on how you define important. That is a purely subjective judgment."

If it was possible to throttle a machine, that is exactly what Mitchell would be doing right now. Instead, he took a deep breath of the richer o2 levels and reformulated the question. "Is it time-sensitive? Relevant to the safety of the ship or myself? Does it substantively change the nature or direction of our mission?"

Again, a momentary delay. "No."

"Then I guess it wasn't important, was it?"

While he was up, he might as well get something to eat. The food substitutes weren't especially tasty, but at least eating helped pass the time between asteroid scans. True space exploration consisted largely of boredom.

"Your grandfather Peter Shabagwis has died." Mitchell stopped breathing for a second. "Although this news does not fall under any of the categories you mentioned, I believe—based on my knowledge of human nature—it can still be classified as 'important.' Am I in error? I ask only in case a similar situation should arise in the future. I believe you have another grandfather back on Earth, and one remaining grandmother."

Papa Peter was dead. This was such a surprise. Although Papa Peter had been well into his eighties, Mitchell thought Papa Peter would outlive him and everybody in the family. He was that kind of man. Old but not infirm. Aged but not weak. Slow but still sharp. And just damn tough. Now he was no more, while Mitchell floated out here, farther away than the old man could ever imagine. Part of him wished Mac had not woken him with this announcement.

"No, Mac, you did the right thing."

Disembarking from the chamber, Mitchell immediately felt the resumption of faux gravity, so called because it was a system of magnetic attraction instead of legitimate gravity. A metallic resin added to the material in his clothing interacted with a small magnetic force coming from the deck plates to give a rudimentary sense of gravitational pull. His organs and hair still knew there was in fact no downward drag, but at least the added effort of movement kept his muscle degeneration at about 40 percent of the expected level, meaning longer, less debilitating trips in space.

"Do you need me to do anything?"

Lost in thought, Mitchell shook his head before remembering Mac did not have interior optical sensors. "No thanks, Mac. I'll take it from here."

Papa Peter. His Native grandfather. The only real Aboriginal influence in his life. The remaining two forebears were non-Native, and his mother—Papa Peter's daughter—had died when Mitchell was nine years old. He had only met the man in person a half-dozen times but had felt a certain kinship. His grandfather had always tested him, in positive ways, like making him explain as a child why the universe above was more important than the world below. Once the boy had figured that out and found a way to explain it logically and passionately, his career had been chosen. A good chunk of Papa Peter's philosophy of life could be summed up in a simple sentence: "Step up and represent, or just go home. No room in the middle."

In postings and video chats, the old man had shown a greater interest in Mitchell's life than most of his closer relatives. And when he was first offered these astronomical forays, Peter Shabagwis had been excited for him, maybe even a little envious.

"When I was young, they had just landed on the moon. Such adventures. Bring me back a rock. A pretty one. Maybe it will help me get a girlfriend."

That was in his last video message, a couple days before Mitchell left the confines of Earth. He had not yet found a rock worthy of his grandfather, but he would now, and then he would return to his grandfather's community and lay it on the man's grave. He had a whole asteroid belt to pick from. Yes, it was against protocol for extraterrestrial objects to be handled so casually. Quarantine would definitely be upset. But right now, Mitchell didn't really care. Where he was now, what he was doing, looking for the known in a universe of the unknown and then returning it to what his grandfather's people called Turtle Island for the betterment of everyone—this was the only tribute he could manage for the man.

Back in his quarters, Mitchell searched for the file containing the recorded messages sent to him from Papa Peter, Otter Lake First Nation, Planet Earth. He sat and watched four-and-a-half hours of video messages from his grandfather, sitting in front of the same unremarkable kitchen background, wearing the same baseball cap. Playing back to back the ten years of messages he'd collected during his multiple survey trips, he noticed something that had escaped him in past viewings. He could see his grandfather getting older, greyer, aging with each recording. The man still bubbled with vitality, especially when he laughed, but it was easy to see the passing years etching their signature on his face.

One of his grandfather's last communications got Mitchell thinking. The old man had posed some interesting questions, sitting at his kitchen table, ruminating on his grandson's career. Just idle thoughts about the nature of space travel and Aboriginal identity, two things not usually found together. "Kitchen talk," he called it. If he had looked outside the ship, Mitchell would have seen Ceres, one of the largest asteroids in the solar system, a scant million kilometres or so off the port side. Already well surveyed and picked over, it held no mystery or potential for his mission, but this was a moot point, for the astronaut's mind was back on Earth, sitting in a ramshackle kitchen, enjoying some tea.

"You know, I was thinking about you the other night. I couldn't sleep, so I went outside and looked way up into the heavens. I knew in a few weeks you would be up there somewhere going about your job, just like I am down here in my little cabin, washing the dishes. Boy, when I was a kid I used to think the store, with all its candy, was so far away. I had to walk so far to lose all my teeth. I guess we learn things all the time, huh?"

For a moment the old man's eyes grew distant, but then the lopsided smile Mitchell knew so well returned.

"I want you to think about something. Everything I was taught about being Anishinabe was tied to the land. Everything we were, everything we did came from our relationship to this chunk of earth our people stand on. I know you weren't raised much with our traditions, but I like to think somewhere deep inside you is a fair-sized chunk of Anishinabe, just like those expensive minerals you look for in all those rocks way up there. Maybe that's why you're so handsome."

Now it was Mitchell's turn to smile.

"But being Native in space... Now that's a head-scratcher. Think about it. We sprang from Turtle Island. The earth and water are so tied to who we are. There's an old saying, 'The voice of the land is in our language.' But what happens when you aren't able to run your fingers through the sand along the river? Or walk barefoot in the grass? Or feel the summer breeze blowing through your hair? Nothing natural, only manufactured things around you. Manufactured water, manufactured food, manufactured air. Even manufactured gravity. I understand you even got a manufactured friend up there to talk to. I know that everything we are we carry inside us, but I can't help wondering if it's possible to be a good, proper Native astronaut. Sometimes I get weird thoughts, huh?"

Mitchell froze the image of Papa Peter on his monitor and let his grandfather's smile hover continuously a few feet from his face. Maybe the old man was right. The few things Mitchell had picked up from the elder did seem to contradict everything the astrosurveyor did. First and foremost, no matter how hard he tried, he just could not see Papa Peter, who had dressed perpetually in jeans and denim or plaid shirts, up here in the coveralls Mitchell had been issued. He might have been allowed to keep his baseball cap, though. Nor could the young man imagine his grandfather eating the food, which was bland no matter how much the Mineral Cops tried to liven up the meals. Papa Peter would probably have said there was "never enough salt in this stuff you call food!"

But it was the broader implications his grandfather had brought up that raised uncomfortable and complicated issues. Papa Peter burned sage every morning to greet the new day and honour the Four Directions. So many things in Mitchell's current environment made that simple practice impossible. He might be allowed to bring sage on board, but he certainly couldn't light it in this oxygen-enriched atmosphere that had rather severe and unforgiving fire-suppression technology. Half a second after he ignited the sage, the entire ship would be breathing a distasteful and obnoxious fire retardant that had been sprayed into the ventilation system. It would take days to get rid of the smell.

And there was no dawn or rising sun. The sun never moved, except to recede into the distance. The ship's chronometer told him when "dawn" was, but that was an arbitrary choice by headquarters. Of course, Mitchell could rationalize things however he wanted. He remembered an old saying stating that home is where you hang your hat. Well, dawn could be whenever you got up. The problem was that when you started rationalizing too many things, the significance of the original action was diminished.

Also, how was it possible to honour the Four Directions when there were none out here? No north, south, east or west. Just the endless, horizonless expanse of space. There was a planetary plane, even a galactic plane, but that was rationalizing things again. Some Aboriginal nations in North America believed there were actually Seven Directions: the original four, plus up, down and wherever you were standing. Up and down complicated things even further, but Mitchell was still fairly confident he knew where he was on that seventh direction. One out of seven... not a particularly good batting average.

Other bits and pieces of conversations with Papa Peter came flooding back. The man gave thanks to Mother Earth and Father Sky on a regular basis... This was another difficult reckoning. Mother Earth was very far away. In fact, Mitchell was closer to the backside of Mother Mars—if a planet named after the god of war could be given such a maternal designation. As for Father Sky, it all depended on how you defined sky. Blue, filled with oxygen, nitrogen and various trace elements, with clouds and high-flying birds? Or simply everything above Mother Earth? It was all getting so complicated.

Sitting in a storage locker back on Earth—he could even remember exactly where he had gingerly leaned it against a side wall—was the hand drum Papa Peter had sent him. Made of moose hide and cedar with a stylized painting of an otter on one side, it was one of Mitchell's most treasured possessions. He had listed it on the content form for objects he planned to bring along on the mission, knowing full well it was unlikely to be allowed. And he was right. First of all, it was made of non-sterilized animal and plant matter. Second, it was bulkier than personal belongings were permitted to be and would therefore take up precious space. Third, it was just weird. Launchport had a thing against weird.

His supervisors and the technicians who serviced the vehicle he toured the solar system in pointed out in very specific terms to the frustrated astrosurveyor that because of the extremely delicate calibration of many instruments on the ship, any unauthorized and unanticipated vibrations within the hull could be catastrophic. Bottom line: no drum and especially no playing the drum.

No sweet grass. Not even a lousy dream catcher. Space was meant for atheists or people with little spiritual inclination, it seemed. But then Mitchell remembered there had been Christian astronauts, Muslim ones, and probably a smattering of other faiths. Delaney, an Irish Catholic woman in his training program, had said all she needed was a cross around her neck and her faith in God, and she was ready to face the universe. Papa Peter would probably say it sounds harder to be a good Native person in space.

"Are you okay? You seem unusually quiet today."

Mac's programmed rising tone at the end of a question usually irritated Mitchell. Today, it barely registered.

Of course he was quiet. Who was he going to talk to? He hadn't reached the point of talking to himself yet. After a month on the mission, to relieve the tedium he had found himself humming songs he remembered from his childhood, but Mac kept asking questions about the function of humming and the meaning of the songs. Mac had been programmed to be interactive as a means of keeping the minds of crew members lively and engaged. Mitchell wished he could find that program in Mac's hard drive and erase it. He knew where he was. He knew what he had signed on for. He didn't need a computer trying to be human. Nobody needed that. Besides, small talk had always annoyed him.

"Is this related to the death of your grandfather?"

Closing his eyes, Mitchell struggled to answer without registering anger. Mac was highly unlikely to be hurt or insulted, but reacting irritably to a machine asking a question was one of the first symptoms of a long-term astrosurveyor losing it.

"Yes, it is, Mac. Could you leave me alone for a while? It's a human thing."

"I understand."

Does it really? Mitchell wondered. Or was that some pre-programmed response?

"But I have taken the liberty of researching your grandfather. I hope that is all right."

The anger was returning. Why would Mac have done that? Mitchell felt almost... violated.

"I thought you might like this. Nine years ago, your grandfather appeared at a National Aboriginal Day celebration in Ottawa. He was part of something called a drum group. I have found thirty-two minutes of archival video of his performance. Would you be interested?"

Mitchell opened his eyes, completely surprised. On the screen was an image of his grandfather sitting around a drum with half a dozen other men. What seemed to be hundreds of people, a mixture of Native and non-Native, were gently swaying and singing along with the traditional song. The familiar skyline of the nation's capital stood proudly in the background.

He had never really understood the nature of traditional Anishinabe music, its words and meanings, but that was indeed his grandfather swinging the drumstick, being as Native as Native could be. Mitchell even recognized a few of the other men seated beside Papa Peter from his occasional visit to Otter Lake. The only problem was the silence. Drum music wasn't silent. As his grandfather once said, it needs to be heard, celebrated, felt and sung to. Instead, all Mitchell heard was the sterile hiss of the ship's constantly recycled air.

"Mitchell... You are still silent. Did I do something wrong?"

"No. No, just unexpected. Thank you."

Kindness and concern from a computer? This was not the kind of service he expected from Mac out here cruising the asteroid belt.

"Perhaps you would like to listen?"

Nodding before he spoke, Mitchell focused the view screen on his grandfather. "I sure would, Mac, but you know the acoustic restrictions."

"I believe you were issued headphones upon assignment to this ship."

Again, surprise. Mac was right. Somewhere in one of his service lockers were headphones. Standard equipment but rarely used. Since each ship usually held only one crew member, there was little need for the privacy that headphones provided. Mitchell listened to a lot of music, but the feeds had been specially modified to not agitate the ship's sensors. For a true audiophile, it was sacrilege, no different than serving a tofurkey at

Thanksgiving. Feeling eagerness for the first time in a long time, Mitchell manoeuvred himself around in his compartment, opening one locker after another. His mission now was to find the headphones.

"I believe you'll find them in the compartment right above the door-lock display."

Once again, Mac was right. Mitchell's appreciation for the computer was growing.

"Mac, you are a lifesaver." Mitchell plugged them into the proper input.

"A bit of an exaggeration, but I will accept the compliment. Enjoy."

"Thanks, Mac." Mitchell felt real gratitude to the automated voice and programmed personality.

"All in a day's work. I will take care of business while you mourn."

Putting the headphones on, Mitchell could hear Papa Peter's voice rising above the others' and feel the pounding of the drum. He could feel everything his grandfather was washing over him. It was good. Song after song made him realize that even though he was only one quarter Anishinabe, he could be fairly confident he was the only Anishinabe out here in the asteroid belt, possibly the only one outside of Earth and the three space stations. This was the only drum music for millions and millions of kilometres. This was a responsibility.

As his grandfather used to say, he'd better step up and represent, because he was a hell of a long way from home. Mitchell started humming, his fingers beating a rhythm on the plastic console.

As promised, Mac watched over Mitchell as he visited with his grandfather.

DREAMS OF DOOM

I know this will make me sound like I'm crazy, but I'm not. At least I hope not. Everything I am about to tell you is true, no matter how crazy it may sound. I can hear them approaching, so I will have to be quick. I don't know how long this will stay online, but hopefully, by God's or whoever you may believe in's grace, these few minutes are enough to get the story out. A few minutes is better than no minutes. Read this as fast as you can. Print it out if possible. Spread the word any way you can.

My name is Pamela Wanishin and I work... used to work... for a small Aboriginal newspaper called the *West Wind*, located in Otter Lake, a small Ojibway community in Central Ontario. We covered the usual political, social and environmental bullshit that happens in First Nations communities and the larger Aboriginal political universe. Nothing extraordinary or particularly award-winning. Just the minutiae of Aboriginal life. In the world of investigative journalism, we were hardly a threat.

Of course, that was when the *West Wind* still existed. Three days ago, our funding was mysteriously cut. Asbestos was found in our building, which is odd since it was built fifteen years after asbestos was banned. Four of our staff are in jail. Two reporters for possessing four kilos of weapons-grade nuclear fuel, found in a large gutted deer hanging to cure in their backyard. Two other employees for wanting to join ISIS. One-way plane tickets to Turkey were found in their underwear drawers. And one intern is missing. The authorities say they have evidence she was selling government secrets to foreign powers. Strange when you consider she didn't know the difference between Australia and Austria. But the government is never wrong, right? I'm all that's left... And I don't know for how long.

First things first. Four days ago, a package arrived at our office. Sally, our part-time combination reporter/receptionist/IT person—a proud Mohawk woman we were told planned to travel to the Middle East to become a jihadi's bride—dropped it on my desk with a thud.

"It says 'Editor.' I guess that's you." Our job titles were kind of loosey-goosey, and it was Thursday, making me the editor.

The plain, medium-sized package looked so innocuous. Brown wrapping paper, almost like butcher's paper, no label, no return address, just our address in a childish, hurried scrawl. Sally looked on as I removed the packaging. Inside a small cardboard box, I found what appeared to be a broken and crushed dream catcher, with a thumb drive.

"How peculiar," was Sally's reaction.

The mystery was mounting. The reporter in me was intrigued. Mysterious packages from unknown sources didn't usually arrive with a thump on my desk.

"Well, let's take a look" was Sally's suggestion.

Otter Lake is an Ojibway community, but for various reasons, Sally found her way here and became the community Mohawk. There are very few jobs where being nosy, bossy and clever is actually an asset. Working at a small monthly newspaper is one of them. Looking back, it's nearly impossible for me to picture her in a burka, subservient to some overbearing, narrow-minded guy with a rifle, eating hummus and figs. Sally didn't like any of those things. Most Mohawk women wouldn't. Actually, most Native women wouldn't embrace that lifestyle, not for all the bannock in the world. But the authorities found incriminating emails and a dress pattern for a burka in her bottom drawer, amid all her sweatpants and thongs.

"Okay," I agreed, and plugged the thumb drive into my computer. My first mistake.

It took about three seconds for it to open and the files to download. Wow, I thought. There were a lot of them. All different kinds. Most seemed to be tech files, dealing with harmonics and frequency modulation. Others were schematics of antennas and crystal vibration rates. And then there were the reports on testing and research, many bearing the logo of Indigenous and Northern Affairs Canada. I scanned as quickly as I could, until I heard Sally's voice again.

"Okay, I'm bored." The future enemy of the state stepped outside to have a cigarette.

Our newspaper had already been put to bed, as we say in the business, ready to be sent out to the printers. So I had some spare time to look this stuff over. Everything that popped up on my screen was puzzling. And what was it doing at our newspaper? We had a few discreet stringers who worked for the government, and they were good for the occasional leak or substantiated rumour, but this seemed a little out of our league. Still, I was hooked. I read and read. It was late in the day, and I was happy for something interesting to make the remaining time pass quickly. I was barely conscious of Sally and the rest leaving for the night as I sat there, reading file after file, and then rereading them. Comparing some of the test reports with the anticipated results. Some of these reports were decades old; others were dated just a month ago. Whatever these people were up to, it had been a long time in the planning. But I'm getting ahead of myself… It seemed this was important enough for somebody to steal all these files, most of which were clearly marked "Classified," and then send them to me. But why me? Why the *West Wind*? And what the hell did a trashed dream catcher have to do with anything?

By about ten that night, after I'd gone through just a small portion of the files, the accumulation of information I had so far amassed was beginning to answer a good number of my questions but also to generate quite a few more. And the answers were not pleasant. In fact, they were horrifying.

Finally aware of my growing hunger and the waning hours, I went home, clutching my computer and the thumb drive closely. Above my bed hung a small, unassuming dream catcher that an aunt had given me three years ago when I got my job at the *West Wind*. I set myself up on my bed with a bowl of day-old hangover soup and some tea, the dream catcher hanging over me as I continued to pore over the files. Each successive file made me increasingly uncomfortable. Looking back and forth from the construction schematics on my screen to the dream catcher over my right shoulder, I was struck by a realization. The dream catcher's circular construction, with the hole in the middle of the lacing, resembled an eye. Not knowing what else to do, and feeling a bit silly, I put the dream catcher in a drawer in the spare room down in the basement.

I live alone now, ever since Larry and I broke up a couple months back, in a house I rent from my uncle. It's kind of small, just the essentials, near the lake and pretty isolated. When you spend all day working in an office and talking with people on the phone or in person, you learn to treasure your alone time. Upon reflection, that may have been a bad decision. Living alone, unfortunately, means living alone, by yourself, nobody else. I was a good quarter-kilometre from anybody else, looking at what I was sure were classified files. Maybe this level of intelligence is why I never rose above middle management.

I fell asleep. Like a bad acid trip, dream catchers of all different sizes and designs paraded through my unconscious mind. I remember several chasing me, dive-bombing me like rabid eagles.

I woke with a start the next morning, my head buried under a pillow for protection. After a brief internal debate, I decided to call Sally and tell her I wasn't feeling well. With the paper already finished for the month, it would be a slow week anyway, and I thought a day finishing up that voluminous list of files might be more productive.

Still in my jammies, I prepared a plate of toast with peanut butter and another cup of tea. I grabbed the notepad I'd been jotting down notes on and began to leaf through it, refreshing my mind and confirming what I had read, not dreamt, the night before.

Looking through the warren of files and charts, one phrase had kept coming up. Project Nightlight. What an odd term. I knew what a night light was. I had one for years as a child after a bat found its way into my bedroom one night. It wouldn't protect me against bats, but at least I would be able to see them coming. But Project Nightlight… What the hell was that? As the reporter's adage dictates, when in doubt, Google. It was a mistake that would come back to haunt me.

I typed the two words into the rectangular box and pressed the return key. The search engine searched. And searched some more. A good twenty or thirty seconds passed with nothing much happening. I tried again, but now my keyboard seemed uninterested in what my fingertips were telling it. My laptop had frozen. Then, a second later, the screen went dead. Two seconds later, the power in the entire house went down. Three seconds later, my heart was pounding in my chest. Normally I can believe in coincidence, but not that day.

Living in the country, you get used to power failures. I had a supply of candles and flashlights hidden somewhere for just such an emergency. But there were no thunderstorms anywhere in the area. The sun was streaming in through my kitchen window. My first thought—or prayer—was that maybe somebody had hit a hydro pole or something. It had been known to happen. Growing increasingly nervous, I looked out my window and could see Clyde and Shelley's house on the other side of the small bay. I could see their porch light was still on, and so was the flashing marque at the gas station near the highway, so there was still electricity flowing into the reserve. It seemed only I had no power. I took out my cellphone. "Network unavailable."

Every reporter, whether they work for some supermarket tabloid, a city newspaper or a Native paper, harbours a certain amount of paranoia. It comes with the job. Mine, by now, was no longer "a certain amount." It was raging like teenage hormones on prom night. Over the last ten hours, I had been reading as much as I could cram into my brain. And I had developed a few conspiracy theories about what all that info meant, with the comfort and safety of knowing nothing like that ever really happens. Especially in Otter Lake. Yet another mistake I made.

As I searched my kitchen drawers for a flashlight so that I could go down into the basement to check the breakers, my cellphone blurbled, a sort of half-hearted ring. It glowed, seeming to have a life of its own. Picking it up, I could see an app downloading. By itself. What little I knew about cellphones told me they are not supposed to do that. Finally, it stopped. Download complete. A moment or two passed as I watched the phone, waiting for it to come to life and declare its sentience. Instead, it rang, normally this time. However, the image on the screen indicated it was a Skype call. I didn't have Skype on my phone. But now it seemed I did. What an uncomfortable coincidence.

Very, very hesitantly, I pressed the answer button. One of the few times in my life I hoped it was some telemarketer calling. Standing in the dark of my house, I said hello.

There was no response. No image on the screen either. So much for Skype. Again, I talked to the phone in my hand. "*Ahneen.* Is anybody there?" I don't know why I said hello in Ojibway. No Ojibway I know would know how to do anything remotely close to this.

Still no response from my once best friend, now an alien phone, though I thought I could hear the sound of slight movement. Of course, it could have been my imagination. At that point, I think I would not have been surprised if Frankenstein's monster, the Wolf Man, the Terminator and the prime minister of Canada had all poured into my living room. That, I probably could have handled. But this, the not knowing, the mystery—this was pure hell. I do not do creepiness well.

"Okay, I'm hanging up."

"Hold on. One second please. I can't read as fast as I once could."

It was a voice. A man's. Older. Educated. He sounded white and slightly distracted.

I was way too uncomfortable for such a beautiful morning. "Who are you?"

I heard the man clear his throat. "Okay, I think I'm up to speed. My apologies. You took us quite by surprise, and I had to scan a lot of material in a remarkably short period of time. How's the weather out there? It looks like we're expecting a storm by mid-afternoon."

This man seemed to be an awfully polite mystery. Everything about this whole thumb drive incident was throwing me off.

"No clouds." I didn't know what else to say.

"Ms. Wanishin, I believe…"

"How do you know my name?"

"Oh my, that would take far too long to go into. Let's just say… I work for the government. But enough about me, let's talk about you."

I did not want to talk about me. Most definitely I did not want that. Everything was wrong. I was standing in my kitchen, in my jammies, talking to somebody from the government who had managed to hack into my cellphone. Only the day before I had been transcribing audio from the band council meeting, the most hated part of my job. Never thought I'd miss doing that.

I put my phone on speaker and set it down on the counter, beside the empty Shake 'n Bake box from Tuesday's dinner, and backed away. I knew the device itself wasn't the problem, but I still didn't want to be touching it.

"It's about the thumb drive, isn't it?"

There was a small chuckle at the other end. The voice sounded well mannered, even amiable. "Well, I guess even that much must be obvious. Yes, it seems somebody in our department has been very naughty and peed in our Rice Krispies. We believe we know who it is and are in the process of taking steps to deal with the leak, if you'll pardon the pun."

"And what department would that be?" Even under stress, the reporter in me came out.

"Let's just say I work in a special branch of Indigenous and Northern Affairs Canada. You wouldn't know the name. It's rather hush-hush. And please, pick up your phone and hold it properly. I really don't like looking at your ceiling. Especially in the dim light."

Suddenly, the lights in the house came on. Just like that.

"Ms. Wanishin, the cellphone please…?"

If creepiness was like a light, I would have been blind by then. I did as the man asked and picked up my phone, looking directly into its blank screen. My house had never felt more empty or remote.

"That's better. Now I can see you properly."

"I can't see you."

"Well, that's probably for the best. What you don't know can't hurt you, as they say. How I look is unimportant. I am just a nameless and faceless cog in the grinding wheels of bureaucracy. A true minion. Sad but accurate. And as such, the less that is known about me the better. But regarding you, Ms. Wanishin, it seems we have a problem. And by extension, so do you."

I forced out a question. "What department?"

"I'm sorry?"

"What department of Indigenous Affairs do you work for? I know them all."

"Ah, I remember taking philosophy in university and always being startled by the humongous difference between what people think they know and what they actually know. What you don't know, Ms. Wanishin, is far greater than what you do know. Still, I don't suppose there would be a problem in telling you we are an undisclosed, rather unheralded but important branch, kept off the books, you could say. Only a handful of people within the government know of our existence. We work best in the shadows."

At that moment, my life was nothing but shadows. "What's your charter? Your mandate?"

Once again, I heard his small chuckle. "My, you are the intrepid little reporter, aren't you? Why should I tell you? I'm sure telling you what little

I already have has bent our rules somewhat. But I like you, Ms. Wanishin, I do. And I am sorry to have put you in this difficult position."

"What difficult position?" I tried to swallow my fear. "I'm in trouble, aren't I?"

This time, I heard the man sigh. An exhalation full of regret and reluctance. I found myself looking out the kitchen window at my lilac-bordered driveway, the outline of my car urging me to run. Shoes, I thought. It might be prudent to put on shoes and grab a coat. I had an uncomfortable feeling about where the rest of this conversation and day were going. I tried to keep the cellphone positioned so that this guy, whoever he was, couldn't tell what I was doing. For that reason, I chose to slip into flats since I didn't have to tie them.

"I am afraid so. Through no fault of your own, you have come to possess some classified information that for the safety of our country cannot be allowed to be disseminated to the public. Obviously, with you being a reporter, there is a conflict there, as I am sure you can see. It, therefore, requires that we take immediate action."

"Project Nightlight, right?"

"Right, Project Nightlight. Those two words will be the final two nails in your coffin, I am sorry to say."

"Literally or metaphorically?"

Once more there was a pause. "Literaphorically. How about that?" Then the man laughed at his own joke. I hate people like that.

"I should not have Googled it. That's how you found me, right?"

"Yes. We have a rather sophisticated search program keeping an eye out for certain words and phrases that may pop up on the internet or in the media. This was a serious red flag. We knew there were a number of classified files that had been surreptitiously downloaded, but why, by whom and for whom... that was still under investigation."

"Are you going to kill me?" I couldn't believe I was in a situation where I had to say those words.

"Let's worry about that tomorrow. Right now..."

"You're coming to get me."

"My dear, we're almost there."

Dropping the phone, I grabbed my computer and the thumb drive. I flung open my front door, departing from the once secure and safe embrace of my home of three years.

"Ms. Wanishin, I really don't think——"

The door closing behind me ended my part of the conversation. Six large running steps across my side patio and driveway and I was opening the door to my car, planning to drive as fast and as desperately as I could in whatever direction offered me the best chance of safety. I had the key in the ignition and my pumping heart in my throat when logic managed to fight its way through my panic.

They—whoever they were—would more than likely be expecting a car chase. How else but by road would they be getting here? I didn't like where this was taking me. I couldn't drive my way to safety. I had to use Plan B, except I didn't have a Plan B. Small-time reporters from obscure First Nations don't often have need of a Plan B.

I was dangerously close to hyperventilating when I realized I might actually be in possession of a Plan B. Getting out of the car, I ran down to the lake and along the shoreline. My cousin Walter had a motorboat stored at a dock five minutes away, or one minute at full gallop.

Every step I took along the lakeshore, I was sure somebody would leap out of the bulrushes and tackle me. Instead, I startled about half a dozen creatures that had settled down in the bushes for a lazy summer afternoon. My shoes had half filled with sand and water before I finally found the boat. Luckily, Walter always left it with a full tank of gas. Another fifty metres farther along the water's edge, I could see his house, with his three kids playing on the deck, unaware of the evil in the world. I envied them.

I leaped into his boat. He'd upgraded his boating preferences since I'd last gone out with him a few years back. And it had been a few more years since I had personally operated a vessel designed to travel through water, but I still remembered the fundamentals. When I was a teenager, I'd worked with my uncle as a fishing guide. I was pretty sure the technology of nautical travel hadn't changed substantially. I primed the engine, pushed the right button and roared out into the wide embrace of Otter Lake.

As I travelled deeper into the islands that peppered this side of the lake, I looked over my shoulder. From halfway across the water, I could see cars, maybe four or five, converging on my house from both sides. I knew they could hear the boat—sound travels amazingly well across calm water—but a variety of boats could be seen scattered across the lake, all moving in different directions.

Still dressed in my pyjamas, flats and raincoat, I made my way through the islands, navigating from memory. I was looking for Joshua Red's cabin.

He was a friend of the family about my age who loved to get away from the hustle and bustle of reserve life by retreating to a small island where his family had built a cabin. He'd been in a car accident several months ago and was still recovering. I knew the cabin was empty and where it was located. More importantly, it was off the grid. Electricity over here was only a theory. Off the grid was good. Off the grid was necessary. Off the grid gave me time to figure things out.

There were cottages and cabins strewn throughout the dozen or so islands, so it would take them time to connect the dots and find me. Hopefully, I would have a Plan C by then.

As I expected, the cabin looked empty but at the same time welcoming. I hid the boat behind a patch of bulrushes and went in. I hadn't been there in a few years, but as far as I could tell, nothing had changed. The winds of fashion and renovation don't often blow across the watery expanse of Otter Lake. Once I had closed the door behind me, I slid to the floor. My fast breathing was making me nauseous, and it quickly gave way to sobbing. I couldn't believe what was happening to me. Pamela Wanishin, fugitive. Movies about dogged reporters flashed across my consciousness, albeit with an Aboriginal flavour: *All the Prime Minister's Men*, *Ojibway Holiday*, *The Blue Heron Brief*, *The Girl with the Orca Tattoo*. Maybe I was having a psychotic episode.

Struggling to get up off the floor, I noticed a dream catcher hanging in the window. There was another one against the far wall. Knowing they were somehow tied into this whole mess, I tore them down and ripped them apart. I would apologize to Joshua later… I hoped.

There were still a lot of documents left to go through. At the moment, I was safe and I had three, maybe three-and-a-half hours of power left on my computer. All good wars need weapons and a battle plan. I had a feeling they existed somewhere in those electronic files. The day stretched on as I read, my little corner of the cabin lit only by the flickering screen of my computer. The sun and my computer's battery gave out about the same time. I sat in darkness for the longest time, putting all the pieces together, or trying to.

My head rested sideways on the Formica table, deep in a troubled sleep, until the early morning sun decided it was safe to make an appearance. For the second morning in a row, I awoke with a jerk. Long hours of contemplation had helped me figure it all out before sheer exhaustion gave me a few hours of solace. One document led to another, which explained a third, which confirmed a fourth and made sense of a fifth. The whole thing was huge... we're talking national media huge.

But first it was morning, and with all the excitement and exertion I was now hungry. The ever wise and prepared Joshua had several cans of soup and stew on his shelves, probably several years old. Not my normal morning yogurt and berries, but these were not normal times. I mulled my options over as I forced down some lukewarm beef stew and dreadful instant coffee. It was all so bizarre. Obviously I had to get this thumb drive and all its information to somebody with more resources than a cabin on an island stocked with canned food older than my shoes. I should have gone into nursing like my mother had wanted.

For the rest of that day I held the thumb drive close in my hand, pondering how such a tiny, innocuous device could have such vicious consequences. I watched boats pass by the island, convinced the occupants were scanning the treed canopy for a thirty-year-old Ojibway reporter who, through no effort of her own, had fucked up her life and had no idea how to repair it. Across the calm waters I could see the community of Otter Lake, the thin treeline in the hazy distance. What was going on there, I found myself wondering.

Those were the longest and loneliest two days of my life. I lived off two cans of ravioli, one box of uncooked Kraft Dinner and what I think was a granola bar. Every moment, I expected government officials to jump out of the poison ivy or leap up from the water lilies. With only my own paranoia as company, I was pretty miserable. Add to that the fact that I was alone and confused, and I didn't know what to do. Sleep came at the end of each day, offering refuge but providing only nightmares.

On these islands, there are a lot of birds. Especially crows. They nest all up and down the islands, but during the day they fly over to the community of Otter Lake to look for food, the local garbage dump being the avian restaurant of choice. Early on my third morning at Joshua's cabin, the crows should have been just waking up. Instead, they were already loud and complaining. Complaining about what? Crows don't have many natural enemies, except humans. Seemed we had that in common.

It was around that time that I heard a faint humming, which was gradually growing stronger, and closer. Like a hummingbird on steroids. Looking out the window, at first I couldn't see anything. Then, just above a bunch of sumac trees, I saw some movement. It seemed to flutter and dodge through the thick foliage. I knew what it was instantly. I'd seen them on television, and once, in town, some kid was playing with one in a park. It was one of those drones. It seemed to be sweeping through the woods, looking for something. Looking for me.

"Shit," I muttered.

For a brief moment the morning before, I had hoped I was over-reacting, that this situation I found myself in wasn't as dangerous as I had thought. But what was slowly moving toward the cabin was definitely not some rich kid's toy. Even from this distance I could tell it was all decked out with instrumentation and things I couldn't even begin to identify. How had it found me, alone on a small island kilometres away from where I was supposed to be? Nevertheless, it was time to go—again.

I left the computer behind and grabbed the thumb drive. I opened the front door, ready to make a dash for the boat… then I realized there wasn't much point. That thing could fly faster than I could run, and faster than a twenty-year-old boat and a twelve-horsepower motor could travel. I backed into the cabin, trying desperately to figure things out. The humming was louder now, practically overhead. Cautiously, I looked out the only window that had a bare approximation of curtains, actually moth-eaten dish towels. I couldn't see the drone, but through the pathway to the dock I could see an island about a half-kilometre to the east. And I was pretty sure I could see another drone over there. Evidently, they were combing all the nearby islands. This was not good. This was way above this Native reporter's pay grade.

I could hear the drone circling the cabin. I also heard a floorboard creak beneath my foot. Joshua suddenly became my favourite family friend for the second time. For "emergencies," as he called them, the man often kept a rifle hidden under the floorboards. Just a .22 but enough to scare off hungry but skittish bears and coyotes. He had shown it to me once, when we were celebrating his twenty-fifth birthday. Moving quickly, I pulled it and a box of shells out from their hiding spot under the floor. I loaded it clumsily—twice I dropped the shells—and charged through the door, turning around as I cleared the roof. Instantly I could see it, turning to face me. I lifted the gun, aimed, pulled the trigger and stepped backwards, reacting to the recoil. I had missed.

Putting another shell in, I took my time. The drone began to rise, as if sensing the danger. Taking a deep breath, I squeezed the trigger, this time anticipating the recoil. As if God were answering a prayer for the first time in my life, I saw the back left horizontal blades fly apart. It dipped to the right, trying to compensate, but with little luck. In front of it was a rather large cedar tree that proved to be substantially more obstinate than the drone. No more drone.

Strangely, I did not feel elated. I knew I had only bought myself a few minutes, maybe ten at best. It had seen me. But again, I had to ask myself, how had it found me? And how had it known someone was in the cabin? Then the answer came to me—thermal imaging. Environment Canada often used the same thing to check out deer populations in densely forested regions. I was the warmest thing on the island. And the largest. That thing, even in its dozen pieces, looked like it had every possible surveillance toy on it. It was enough to make my little nephew Evan, who loved all those realistic war video games, wet his pants. But how do you fight thermal imaging?

Camouflage! If my body heat stood out so noticeably on this deserted island, then give it something else to look at... or hide behind something hotter. Dropping the rifle, I began to put my plan into effect as quickly as a handful of dry crackers and one cup of black instant coffee would allow me. I'd lost track of whether this was Plan c or d, but so far I was alive, so I decided not to break the chain of theoretical backup plans. I grabbed some of my cousin's kerosene lamps and a quarter jug of gas he had stored under the awning beside the door, and doused the cabin and nearby trees. I hated what I was doing. Joshua would also hate what I was doing. This went against everything I believed in. I had spent many happy days swimming and playing here as a kid, but what else could I do? Taking most of the gas from the spare tank in the boat, I soaked some of the trees close to it. Already I could hear more drones approaching, their buzz slightly louder than bees.

Taking a deep breath, I ignited a barbecue lighter I'd found in the cabin. Handy little things—darn clever, those white people. I saw a drone coming toward me over the sumac bushes as I lit the trail of gas. For the longest moment in the world, I was sure something was wrong, because there was no corresponding whoosh of several gallons of gasoline bursting into flames. Maybe the ground and trees were too wet from morning dew. Maybe I didn't know as much about setting an island on fire as I'd thought.

Then suddenly, the path and the bushes alongside it erupted in flames. Running like a dog after a cat, the fire raced up the path and then attacked the cabin and surrounding forest. Almost instantly, the island was on fire. And I was still standing on it. Quickly I got into my boat as the new drone moved closer, hovering almost directly over a group of dry bushes I'd drenched just a few moments earlier. Behind it I saw the fire racing down from the cabin along the other side of the path until it was directly under the drone. A sudden whoosh of flames and the drone, blind and damaged, crashed into the water not more than three feet from my boat. By the time I was a kilometre offshore, the whole island was ablaze.

I was sure I could see two other drones circling the island, dodging back and forth. At first I was afraid they'd spot me out on the still water of the lake, but by then, with all the early morning fishermen plying their trade, people fleeing nearby islands and billowing smoke creating an amazingly effective smokescreen, I was effectively lost in the confusion. It looked like I would live to fight another day.

By the time I pulled up onshore at Otter Lake, I knew what I needed to do—sort of. First of all, I needed help. So far, God, the Creator, Lady Fortune or random chance had taken a shine to me, but I knew that without other forms of help, I would not continue to be so lucky. Leaving the boat, I made my way through the village, waving casually to people emerging from their houses to see the burning island across the bay. Passing two friends, Mike and Charlie who worked at the gas bar, I noticed them looking at me curiously. It was then I became acutely aware that I was still dressed in my soggy pyjamas, slip-on shoes and a raincoat, smelling like gasoline and three days on an isolated island. By this point, I didn't give a shit.

My nephew Todd from the snack shack drove by. He waved to me. I saw his car had a dream catcher hanging from its rear-view mirror, as did the three cars that followed his. I passed my Aunt Julia's house. I saw a large dream catcher in the window. The elementary school had a big one painted on its side. The conspiracy, right under my nose, was enormous. More cars passed with more dream catchers clearly visible.

The dampness of the morning, the trip across the lake and perhaps a certain level of shock were making me shiver on Sally's doorstep. It took a moment for her to answer the door.

"Pamela, where the hell have you been?! Do you know what's been going on around here? We've all been… Ho-ly! What happened to you?" Dressed for work, she looked good, unlike me. "Is something wrong?"

"Can I come in? I need help."

She stepped aside and held the door open for me. Once I was in her house, I felt a certain amount of relief. I flinched, hearing a buzzing, before realizing it was her old refrigerator.

Sally pulled out a chair for me and I gratefully sat down.

Her hospitality gene kicking in, she poured me a cup of coffee. "Did you see the fire across the bay? Isn't that Joshua's island? Is he okay?"

The cup she gave me had the Iroquois two-row wampum sign on it.

"Yeah, he's fi—"

Her cup had a dream catcher design on its side. Dangling over the kitchen sink was yet another.

"Shit," I muttered.

It felt like I was surrounded. With one hand, I grabbed her coffee mug; with the other, I tore the dream catcher from its mounting and threw them both out the door.

"What the hell? My mother gave me that!"

"Listen to me, Sally. Remember that thumb drive I got on Thursday? My God, was that just a few days ago?"

"That was my favourite mug, too."

"Pay attention. Dream catchers are evil. Part of a government plot to control Native people."

For a few seconds, the only sound in the kitchen was the ticking of the clock above the doorway to the living room.

"Huh?"

"Okay, stay with me. I've just spent the last couple of days plowing through all the information on that thing. I know this is going to sound weird, but it all makes sense. Okay, now follow me. Dream catchers are almost always made with a metal hoop, right? With intricate interlaced threading or wiring extending inwards. And on those threads are usually beads or crystals—"

"I know what a dream catcher looks like."

I could see I was losing her.

"Do you? Do you really? Think about it. What does that sound like? A metal hoop. Wiring. Crystals?"

A frustrated shrug told me I had lost her.

"An antenna! Or even a satellite dish. A lot of the stuff I read in those files was way over my head, but some secret branch of Indigenous Affairs has spent the last twenty-five years developing the technology and dispersing it among Canada's Native population."

More ticking from the clock, and I heard her refrigerator come on again.

"Have you been out on some sort of binge? I mean, you show up here in your pyjamas and raincoat, smelling of gas, looking like you haven't slept for a while, talking about a dream catcher conspiracy to control Canada's Indigenous people. That's a little unusual."

"Under normal circumstances, maybe."

Digging deep in my raincoat pocket, I removed the thumb drive and thrust it tightly into her hand. She looked at it for a second, growing oddly calm. The thin summer scarf she'd been wearing slipped down to reveal a necklace I'd never seen before. Nestled between her collarbones was a delicate gold dream catcher. Sally tucked some of her long black hair behind her right ear. She had matching earrings.

"Those are new," I managed to say.

Speaking in a monotone, she answered, "They came yesterday. Courier. From my mother in Tyendinaga. Very pretty, don't you think?"

"I think they're beautiful. Don't you, Pamela?"

Now I heard the voice that had forced its way into my life just a few evenings ago, this time coming from her table. Her iPad was on and pointed at me. Once again, Skype was activated but there was no return picture.

"Here we were, trying to figure out how to find you and you just show up. It's always hard to anticipate the benefits of luck. We were just planting a suggestion in Sally here, just in case you decided to contact her."

I didn't say anything. I could feel my options quickly slipping away. And the voice just kept talking, so calm and confident.

"You're quite clever, young lady. I will give you that. We've found the gentleman who sent you the thumb drive. Evidently, he was infatuated with both you and your writing. I believe you met him at a political conference some months ago, but the less said about him the better. The here and now is always more interesting than the then and there, don't you agree?"

"Speaking from an Aboriginal perspective, not always." I had finally found my voice.

"Touché, Ms. Wanishin. I stand corrected."

"Was I right?"

The blank screen looked back at me. "About the dream catchers? It's a lot more complicated than that, but I believe you got the gist."

"But why? I assume a lot of time and money went into this... this..." I couldn't find the right word.

"Ah yes, it was inevitable you would ask that. Suppression of Indigenous unrest, young lady. Both urban and rural. Our best scientists designed today's dream catchers as a sort of pacification protocol. We initiated it to help keep the Aboriginal population less… volatile. Simply put, dream catchers, whether they are on walls, windows, rear-view mirrors or jewellery, act as receivers for—let's call them radio waves for the moment, to help eliminate, or at least moderate, the more radical and detrimental social outbursts that on occasion have plagued our country. Truly, we just want our Native people to be happy. And protesting First Nations are not happy people, which in turn aggravates other segments of the population. You see, it's for your own good."

I found myself leaning against the kitchen sink, struggling to talk. "When? How?"

"You look a little perturbed, Ms. Wanishin. Perhaps you should sit down."

I sat down on a kitchen chair with a thump.

"I don't… This is… You can't…"

I looked at Sally, but she hadn't moved. She was still looking down, her gaze unnaturally fixed on the thumb drive in her hand.

"Yes, I realize this is all rather overwhelming. When I first took over this portfolio, I was amazed. You might be surprised to know this was originally put into development right after the rejection of the infamous White Paper. My predecessors could read the writing on the wall, even back then. What with the growing power of the civil rights movement in America, it would only be a matter of time before the same unrest moved north to our little hamlet of freedom. Except, we correctly surmised, it would come from the Native community. We decided to be a little more proactive and discreet than our southern neighbours. Americans can be so over the top, don't you think?"

I thought about the first Trudeau era and the government's attempt to renegotiate the special status of Native people and reserves, basically aiming to politically eliminate us out of any meaningful Canadian existence.

"The White Paper… That was over forty-five years ago!"

"Oh good, you remember your history. Yes, but it was the Oka Crisis that began Project Nightlight. The gradual infiltration of the First Nations community via specially designed dream catchers. That's the beauty of the whole situation. Dream catchers were already becoming all the rage. All we had to do was replace them with our own specially designed ones. You see, we currently have 143 Native women across the country unknowingly pumping out all different variations, sizes, makes and designs of our special dream catchers. We supply them with the proper material and those women alone, specially conditioned by us, supply the vast majority of powwow traders, arts and crafts stores and conference vendors, making saturation of the market total and complete. Of course, there are a few made here and there by random entrepreneurs, children or therapy groups, but they are just a small percentage. The whole operation is remarkably effective."

I tried to stop myself from hyperventilating. He was telling me everything, but why? Because I was trapped and he was amusing himself. If I could have remembered the Lord's Prayer, I would have been saying it then.

"You'll notice that since Oka and Ipperwash, other than a few flareups here and there, things have been relatively quiet. The Idle No More movement was reasonably calm and non-invasive. The Native population, though still vocal and opinionated, has become largely non-violent. Add to that a few apologies here, a royal commission there… and the Canadian government and public shuffle along, dealing with the more important issues of the day. See, a much better, regulated society. And the real beauty of the plan is, for the most part, only those within the target population would want or have dream catchers, and they then voluntarily pass them on to those outside their immediate cultural environments who share similar political and social views. Meaning, of course, that non-Native sympathizers who would be likely to march or protest alongside their Indigenous brothers and sisters are frequently given dream catchers by their Native friends, thus completing the saturation. Brilliant, wouldn't you say? We're very proud."

I looked at the docile Sally and wondered if that was my fate.

"Obviously, your friend needed a rather large dose to ensure her immediate compliance. But as I am sure you would agree, the general Aboriginal population is not even aware that they are being socially massaged. Well, that's how I like to refer to it."

"Socially massaged… How long do I have?"

"For what?"

"Until you socially massage the hell out of me? Or you kill me?"

The man at the other end of the conversation laughed. "My dear Ms. Wanishin, we are not going to kill you. That would be too… American."

"So what are you going to do with me, then? This is not an 'agree to disagree' situation."

He laughed again. "Quite right. You will simply be... removed. To a more secure location for containment. To ensure the continuing calm of Canadian society, you understand. We have a wonderful facility located on Ellesmere Island. You will love it there."

"And Sally? What will happen to her?"

That's when I learned about the decision made by Otter Lake's resident proud Mohawk to move to the other side of the world and humbly embrace a violently patriarchal system.

"I love the irony," the voice commented. "I'm big on irony." Almost gleefully, he told me about his plans for the others at the paper and for the *West Wind* itself. "It's called 'containment and cleanup.' It will be a bit messy, but we can make it work. We have before. These little scenarios are how I exercise my creativity. I know you're not really in a position to appreciate the solution, but maybe someday you'll grow to be amused."

My mind was tap dancing. I have always believed that every problem has a solution. Somewhere in the back of my overtaxed mind, a dim but possible plan was beginning to form. But would I have time?

"I assume you've already got Sally's house surrounded and are ready to move in."

"I wouldn't be very efficient at my job if my people weren't in place already."

"Will you give me a chance to sing my death song?"

Silence. In the quietness, I could almost hear the man's puzzlement. It only lasted a second.

"Death song? The Ojibway don't have a death song. And as I said, you aren't going to be killed."

"I misspoke. I meant my removal song."

I don't know where that idea came from, but I assumed that somebody who was used to being in control, and arrogant, probably had a shallow understanding of Native culture and thought of himself as sympathetic and respectful—in his own way. Also, it might appeal to his penchant for irony.

This time, there were two seconds of silence. I could sense the man's control of the situation flickering, just a bit. "Removal song? Again, the Ojibway—"

Now was my chance.

"Yes, we do. Reserves, residential schools, the Sixties Scoop, prison—we are being removed all the time. It's become part of our contemporary culture. Necessity and tradition dictated that we develop a removal song. Please allow me the cultural consideration to—"

"I am sorry, but we cannot—"

"Then I will burn this house down, thereby causing as much chaos and drawing as much attention as possible, a condition I am sure people in your position hate. I've burned an island to the ground; a house would be a lot easier. What do you say to that, mysterious white guy? All I need is ten minutes. Oh look, lighter fluid…"

If silence could be angry, I thought, his would be screaming. Each second passed with agonizing slowness. I looked out Sally's window and couldn't see anything, but I knew, sure as my ex-boyfriend owes me $1,400, they were there.

"Ten minutes… for your removal song."

I grabbed the iPad on the table and quickly disabled the internet. Then I made sure Sally's cellphone was turned off. To be safe, I took the battery out.

The cool thing about Sally is she did triple duty at the paper— receptionist, IT person and reporter. First thing I did, on the off chance the house was bugged, was start chanting. Random noises and vocalizations. Second thing was I grabbed Sally's voice recorder and turned it on. As accurately as possible, I have recounted everything that has happened to me since hell arrived in a small paper package. Luckily, she also had one of those programs that converts voice to text. Hopefully, that is what you are reading now.

As a small business operating out in the country, the paper often had its own unique difficulties to deal with. Power surges, thunderstorms, spontaneous blackouts that could severely affect internet and phone reception. So Sally, in all her wisdom, saw fit to connect the *West Wind* office to her own house about forty metres down the road with a hard line to ensure none of these problems would interfere with getting the paper out. Being the smart woman she is… or was, Sally even got a grant to pay for it. This meant her server was connected to the server at the paper, with no way for the mysterious white guy to listen in or monitor, unless he physically tapped into the actual cable. He was working on the fly just as much as I was.

The beauty of the situation is I will upload my story and the thumb drive files onto Sally's server, which will immediately send them to the server at the office—with its huge mailing list, website and contact files. As Sally, who is still sitting at the kitchen table looking blankly down at her now-empty hand, explained to me once, if there is a break in power or connection at her end, whatever is loaded on the office's server will automatically be emailed wherever it has been pre-programmed to go. Or from here, if necessary, as a backup. The second they storm this house, I assume they will grab Sally's hard drive in an attempt to secure the evidence. And the minute they disconnect the server I am about to plug the thumb drive into, everything I have just recorded will go international and they'll be fucked. I, too, love irony.

So this is my story. Tell everybody. Do not trust dream catchers, especially ones made from metal hoops, wire and plastic string and beads. They are evil. They are destroying the Native people. Rip them from cars, windows and walls, necklaces and earrings, crush or burn them, wherever you see them. This is the only warning you will get. Fight the dream catcher!

What will happen to me, I don't know... I've always wanted to go to Nunavut, but not—

Oh shit, gotta go...

MR. GIZMO

In a small community, on a tiny island on the edge of a huge ocean, sat a boy. He was not a small boy, nor was he a large boy. He was a medium-sized teenager, fast approaching the beginning of his third decade on Turtle Island but feeling the weight of a thousand years upon his shoulders. In his unremarkable room, he sat on the edge of his unmade bed. Around him was the detritus he had so far acquired in his unmemorable life—a mishmash of outgrown toys, casually read graphic novels, rudely piled clothes—and he held a small .38 snub-nosed revolver firmly in his hand.

The house was empty and quiet. Only the sounds of the island's animal citizens could occasionally be heard filtering into the room from the world outside. Squeezing the wooden handle, the boy could feel the criss-crossed texture of the gun's grip. Lying dead centre in his palm, it felt heavy. Heavier than he had expected, but then it was a sizable chunk of forged steel. It should be heavy. Why he had thought it would be less substantial he wasn't sure. Maybe it was the way it was whipped out and waved about so casually on television and in films that made it seem less formidable. Whatever. Make no mistake, the sheer ominous heft of the six-chambered firearm told him it was an instrument of violent death. He squeezed the handle again, making sure his index finger stayed distant from the trigger. For the moment, anyway.

Seventeen years of walking the planet had landed him here, at this very moment, at this unique juncture of his life. Half of it lived in the big city of Vancouver, the other half a little ways away in this isolated First Nations community bordering the edges of both a continent and an ocean. Today his thoughts ran dark and bleak. You see, the boy was rapidly running out of family to rely on, and as a result, his sense of self-worth was also depleting. His father... dead from what was described as an "incident" in prison. What was it... eleven years ago already? He could barely remember the man who had called him son. The boy was now probably as tall as his father had been when he'd last seen him. But the man whose DNA he shared had become a mere number, one of the thousands of Aboriginal men who dispropor-tionately "enjoyed" the hospitality of Canada's correctional services. And whether he had been guilty or unfairly caged by the dominant culture's so-called "justice system," somewhere in his journey he had become just a memory for the boy and a statistic for some future royal commission.

The boy's mother had disappeared one night while out in the city. Pleas to the police and the media proved ineffective, and the woman stayed missing and was quite likely dead. Now just another name in a much larger tragedy of murdered and missing women. That was when the boy was sent home, to live with his grandparents. In this house. On this island so far away from everything he knew.

He pulled back the hammer of the gun. "Cocked it" was the term he said silently to himself. The boy was dressed in black, having just come back from his grandmother's funeral. Another branch broken off his heavily pruned family tree. He'd read somewhere that cocking it reduced the amount of pressure needed to pull the trigger from five pounds per square inch to two pounds per square inch, making it easier to fire. He could feel the satisfying click as the hammer locked into place.

This island had been home for a little more than seven years. It sure wasn't like Vancouver. And even though he was probably broadly related to everybody in the village, he still somehow felt alone. And his peers let him know it. That he talked with a city accent. That he knew practically nothing about fishing or his people or anything everybody else found interesting. There were girls he liked who didn't like him. It had been a difficult and lonely seven years. Especially now, with his grandmother buried and his rigorously sober grandfather… now not so sober. The old man had passed out in his room, awash in a rye-and-beer-induced coma. The death of a partner he had shared his life with for more decades than most people live had taken its toll.

So there sat the boy, cradling the gun owned by his grandfather, a gift from an American he had been a fishing guide for a long time ago. Neither he nor his grandfather knew if it had ever been fired.

His grandparents had taught the boy that life was a gift to be treasured. It was now a philosophy the boy had difficulty accepting. In fact, the gun in his hand demonstrated his curiosity about returning that precious gift. He was finishing high school in two months… perhaps a better way of saying it was barely finishing high school, or that high school would be finished with him. What next? University? The thought almost made him laugh. His teachers, though supportive, gave him the impression that would be a waste of time. The fishing industry that abounded in the area? That seemed equally unlikely. It was backbreaking work that required a certain amount of commitment and endurance, neither of which he felt he possessed. Also, embarrassingly, long hours on the open sea made him seasick. Some Kwakwaka'wakw man he was.

All of that added up to a bleak past and an equally bleak future. As the poets would say, it was a shitty life that was seemingly getting shittier. That was the realization that had sent him to the top shelf of his grandfather's closet a little less than half an hour ago. Now in his room, the revolver sat comfortably in his left hand. Slowly, he transferred it to his right hand.

Impulsively, he lifted the gun, extending his arm and looking down the sights of the short, stubby barrel. Aiming. At everything. First, at the poster of some video game his grandparents couldn't afford and whose ancient television probably couldn't process the twenty-first-century technology necessary for him to play it. Still, it was a cool poster. Then, over at the window and the mountain that stood far off in the distance. It was beautiful, dark and distant. Next, on the wall across the room was a mirror with a sullen teenage boy in the middle of its frame. His arm hovered as he looked across the expanse of his room, trying to recognize the person at the other end. The boy was pointing a gun at him, too. Probably as pissed off as he was. Their eyes locked for a moment before both boys slowly lowered their guns.

Finally, on a shelf beside the window, he targeted the centre of his last victim. A toy robot, given to him by his father before he went away. It was an old-fashioned kind of thing, about a foot high, with moving arms and flashing lights. At least, it once had these things. It used to move eagerly across the floor with lights flashing, filling up the world with excited beeps and sirens. Mr. Gizmo—that was what he had once called it. Now it just sat there, gathering dust.

The boy imagined pulling the trigger. The gunpowder igniting, gases instantly expanding. The bullet pushing down the barrel, spiralling slightly, flying across the floor and into the cheap plastic figure. Bits of department store robot parts and made-in-China electronic guts exploding across the room.

"Hey, don't point that thing at me. What did I do?"

Everything in the room stopped. There had been a voice. Definitely a voice. His hand with the gun fell to his lap as he quickly scanned the room. He was alone, as always. He almost dropped the handgun, but when odd and unexpected things happen, perhaps that's an even better time to have a weapon. Door was closed. Cellphone turned off. The only thing the boy could hear now was his own heartbeat.

He did the only logical thing he could think of and asked, "Where...? Who said that?"

No answer. Silence, except for the creaking of the bed as he stood up, turning a full 360 in a second attempt to locate who, or what, had spoken.

Eyeing his old friend warily, the boy approached the toy robot slowly. He leaned in toward the familiar object, studying its worn plastic face and body. The boy hadn't paid this much attention to Mr. Gizmo in a long time. He reached up to his old childhood acquaintance, taking it firmly in his free hand. It wasn't talking. It wasn't doing anything. Just staring back at him, if inanimate objects can indeed stare back.

Not knowing what else to do, he knocked the side of the robot's head with the barrel of the gun—twice. You know, just to be sure.

"You know I can't feel anything. However, I would appreciate it if you wouldn't do that again."

This time, the robot moved. Thanks to a hand opening in surprise and the power of gravity, it plummeted about four feet straight down and then bounced twice on the thick rug. Backing into his dresser, the boy raised his gun, aiming directly at the thing on the floor.

"Who… what the fuck are you?"

There was a very pregnant pause before the boy received an answer.

"If I remember correctly, you used to call me Mr. Gizmo. Never liked that name but also never liked the cheap plastic they made me with. Will you please put that gun down? I know I'm obsolete, but I also know I was not put on Turtle Island to become target practice. I would like my end as a robot to be a little less violent."

Lying face down on the rug, the robot was still. Even if it was indeed talking, it was not moving. None of this made sense. As if to prove his point, the boy continued to point his gun at the toy. At the moment, he was out of other options.

"You! Why… why are you talking? You never talked before."

Sluggishly, as if mired in a dream, the white-and-silver toy managed to roll over onto its back. Its eyes—plastic nodules, actually—were now facing upwards, looking toward the boy and glowing faintly.

"I will tell you if you put the damn gun down."

Although it seemed to the boy that the whole world was spinning around him, he elected not to do as requested.

"Do I look like I'm dangerous? Is this what dangerous looks like to you?"

The boy had to give the robot that. Unless it was one of those Transformer-type things, this toy would have a serious problem overpowering or even hurting him. Almost reluctantly, the boy lowered the gun to his side. But like a jack-in-the-box, it could and would spring forth if needed.

"Now, if you don't mind, can you pick me up and put me back on the shelf? Lying here on the ground gives me a far better view of your crotch than I would like. I would prefer to look you in the eye. Man to man… or robot to teenager, as the case may be."

For a few seconds, neither moved. It seemed Mr. Gizmo was wait-ing patiently, and the boy was assessing the situation. To the best of the boy's knowledge, things like this didn't happen after the funeral of most grandparents.

Suddenly, the robot moved again. Left to right, then right to left, as it struggled against both gravity and a discarded T-shirt that was restricting movement on its right side. "You realize you are making this difficult. Even if I can manage to get upright, there's not a lot I can do from down here." Mr. Gizmo stopped moving. "Well?"

Taking the gun from his grandfather's closet had been the boldest and pluckiest of the boy's limited repertoire of actions. Until now. He could see Mr. Gizmo staring at him, expectantly it seemed. Not knowing what else to do, he grasped his childhood toy in his trembling fingers, ready to drop it, throw it or shoot it if the need arose. But all that was required was to return Mr. Gizmo to his time-honoured location on the shelf. The boy couldn't help noticing how normal the robot's body felt. Not unusually hot or even cold. It wasn't vibrating or tingling. All the boy could conclude was that it felt like any twelve-year-old plastic toy should.

"Thank you. Now, let's talk."

It wanted to talk. It wanted to talk more. It wanted to talk more to him. This couldn't be good. "About… about… what? Talk… about what?"

"Nuclear physics. What do you think? You are standing here, alone in your room, I guess very depressed, with a loaded gun. There aren't a lot of dots to connect."

The gun… The boy had forgotten about the gun still in his hand. Under the circumstances, though, that could be expected. Realizing the situation had changed substantially, he could revisit the need for the gun later perhaps. At the moment, there were other things to consider. He gingerly released the gun, and it landed with a slight thud on a shelf about a foot to the left and just below Mr. Gizmo. Pivoting its head slightly, the robot watched the boy release the weapon.

"Excellent. I think that's progress. Remember that ray gun I used to have? I think you lost that within the first month. Too bad. I always liked that ray gun. But kids, right? They wouldn't be kids if they didn't lose things."

"WHO THE FUCK ARE YOU?"

"I'm Mr. Gizmo, remember? From the planet—"

"Mr. Gizmo never talked. At least, not like this. And not for a long time."

"I've never needed to. Communication is very overrated."

Breathing heavily, his knees dangerously close to buckling, the boy didn't respond. Reality for him was usually constant. Boringly constant, like waves on a beach. Mosquitos in summer. Trips to the bathroom. The only thing in his community that happened on a regular basis was people leaving his life. Not insane incidents like this.

The boy blurted out the words, almost too quickly to be understood. "Then why now? Why… why… why…?" But his confusion seemed to be of no interest to Mr. Gizmo.

"I didn't like where things were going."

Again, the boy tried to coalesce his exploding thoughts. "But how long...? When did...?"

Normally, the boy wasn't verbose. He would get away with as little conversation as he could. But that wasn't the reason he was currently struggling to speak. He fought for the right word to explain what he was trying to express. Then it came to him, though without the necessary grammar or sentence structure.

"Consciousness."

The word had popped into his head, from where he wasn't sure. It wasn't the kind of word used frequently in teenage conversations.

Mr. Gizmo had an answer. "I have always been... conscious, as you put it. Just like you are. Just like your grandfather. Just like your bed. Your bike."

There was so much wrong with that sentence, the boy didn't know where to begin.

"You can't be talking. Am I... am I... crazy?"

Mr. Gizmo, somehow, shrugged his little plastic shoulders. "Well, that's for a toy much more knowledgeable than I am to decide. But enough about me. Let's talk about you."

It seemed his childhood toy wanted to have a detailed and comprehensive discussion with him—about him. Once again, this couldn't be good. His response consisted of a hearty and fearful swallow. Then he managed, "I don't want to talk about me."

"Yeah, but we're going to. Look, I broke protocols to talk to you. At the very least you could be a little more receptive. And grateful. Geez, I bet the Impatient One didn't give the trees this much grief when they showed him the way through the mountains. Or when that carving introduced itself to the Impatient One, who then turned around and adopted it as a brother. At least that carving wasn't so snotty."

Like a drowning man grabbing at a life preserver, the boy suddenly had a frame of reference, albeit one less concrete than he might have preferred. He'd heard that unusual name before, and the references to helpful trees and a carving coming to life tickled the back of his memory. These were stories—fabulous, incredible ones—his grandfather had told him that came from the Kwakwaka'wakw people. His people. What this had to do with a cheap plastic toy named Mr. Gizmo eluded him, though.

"But those are just... just... legends."

"So were the Trojan War and Vikings hanging out on the East Coast. Doesn't mean they're not true. The Impatient One's carving? Distant cousin of mine. Those trees? I knew a gazebo who knew a stump who used to date one of those trees."

More of the traditional tales were slowly coming back, surfacing above the sea of confusion swirling around in the boy's head. He'd listened to them when he was very young, and then again when he was older, relishing their detail and his grandfather's ability to make them feel real. These were stories of the West Coast that had sprung from the mountains and the sea and were first told way back in the epoch known as Time Immemorial. Starring Raven and a plethora of other amazing characters, who until now the boy had relegated to the same status as Santa Claus and Superman.

"Now look, dude, I'm sorry for interrupting your little depression fest here, but I did not like where your interest in that gun was going, and I figured I had to say something. There's been a lot of talk among us about this lately, about where you young people have been going these days. Years, actually. Yeah, ever since the People of Pallor—that's what we call them—arrived, things have been kind of tough for your people. Actually, all First Nations people. Sort of a hangover of the colonized. We call it PCSD—post-contact stress disorder. But, buddy, enough is enough."

"What… what do you… what do you mean, 'There's been a lot of talk'? By who?"

"Us. The things in your life. The things in all Native people's lives. Am I right, or am I right?"

The light on the boy's desk clicked on and off. So did the radio. One of his graphic novels opened a page, and the pillow on his bed seemed to be breathing.

The room around him had been his sanctuary. A fortress where he could contemplate his place in the world and feel reasonably secure. All those years of confident refuge now went flying out the window, which had conveniently just opened itself.

Mr. Gizmo still commanded the floor, or in this particular case, the shelf. "This has got to stop. You were going to kill yourself, weren't you? Or at least you were thinking about it. Come on, admit it. We all saw you."

The amazement he had been feeling, freshly tinged with a healthy dollop of fear, was now replaced by embarrassed surprise intermingled with a substantial dose of shame.

Shaking his head, he muttered, "No, no. I was…"

"Oh, be quiet. We know you better than you know yourself. You were playing with that gun more than you play with yourself."

That substantial dose of shame suddenly became a flood. They had indeed been watching him.

Down the hall, face down on the bed, his grandfather snorted twice, enveloped in a deep intoxicated sleep. If only the old man could be in this room right now, thought the boy. Maybe then there would be answers to the multitude of unasked questions currently crowding the boy's brain. His mother's father had been a treasure trove of cultural facts. Unfortunately, the boy could only remember bits and pieces of what the old man had taught him over the years. Still, above everything else was the Kwakwaka'wakw belief that all things were alive… Actually, "alive" might not be the correct word. Everything had a spirit… Again, that didn't sound right. It was something about everything in Creation being animate—having a will, an intelligence, a state of being. Kwakwaka'wakw stories were replete with tales of objects come to life. If there was a need or a reason, or more specifically, if they wanted to.

"Quit denying it. You were going to kill yourself. What an absolute waste of time and energy. And life. You think life is that depressing? Trust me, that kind of death is even more depressing. Add to that the fact you think the best way to deal with all this is to repaint your grandfather's wall with your brains… Excuse me, but I'm having trouble seeing the logic."

"You don't know—"

Before the boy could finish his sentence, the robot interrupted with a rude beep and a flashing light.

"*I* don't know? Really? You think I don't know? You forget, my morose little friend, I was not born on the date of manufacture printed on my butt. I have been around since the days when Raven used to crash all the parties. I just live here now and go by the name Mr. Gizmo. So, thanks to the passing millenniums, I know a few things."

A sudden thought occurred to the boy. He could just leave. Walk out the door. Leave all this behind and return to a place where the rational laws of reality still operated. Many things in the universe were beyond his understanding—he was bright enough to acknowledge this—and this was definitely one of them. Everything happening now, here, was not normal, and he was rapidly discovering he was a big fan of normal. Normal had become a lot more important and appealing than it had been just five minutes ago. But the doorknob refused to turn, and as a result, the door would not open, despite his furious tugging.

"Have you met my friend the door? We have… an arrangement."

The boy was getting frustrated. He was being thwarted by a cheap, mass-produced toy manufactured in some far-off land.

"You can't hold me prisoner. I have rights."

If a quasi-mechanical coughing sound could be called laughter, the robot had just chuckled loudly. Mr. Gizmo's arm rose, pointing at the boy. "You don't even know what that means. Besides, you were gonna kill yourself, and to the best of my knowledge, dead bodies don't have a lot of rights. So given the choice between a locked door and lying on the floor, staining your grandmother's lovely carpet—which, by the way, is not looking forward to that—I think this is the safest option."

Trapped. The boy knew it. Someday, far in the future, if he survived this exceedingly bizarre encounter, he would look back on the events of today and… well, he had no idea what he would feel or think. True, it takes a certain amount of time and reflection to figure out the complexities of any given situation. And in this particular case, a little therapy might also be required. Still, there were other avenues for the boy to take in search of deliverance.

"I won't do it. I promise. I'll put the gun back."

He wasn't lying. He would do that if the talking robot would let him. Anything, including staying alive, had to be better than being held hostage by a children's toy.

What's even worse than being held hostage by a children's toy? Being lectured to by that same toy.

"Did you know suicide doesn't really solve a heck of a lot? Only those who live forever can really understand that. You might think it's an end to everything that is bothering you. The pain. The misery. All gone in a final act of desperation. But it just transfers the pain, passes it off to other people."

This was all becoming too much for the boy. A talking toy robot that claimed to be a Kwakwaka'wakw spirit lecturing him on mental health.

"How the hell do you know that?"

"Your laptop is my best friend, so we talk. Suicide is really just a permanent solution to a temporary problem. One of the benefits and curses of being eternal is witnessing the history of a people pass by. I was here, in a different form, when the first of the Colour Challenged—that's another thing we call them—landed on these shores. I was here during the epidemics. I was here when the reserves and residential schools were set up. I saw entire generations of your people… shit on. And they survived. And now, you're shitting on yourselves. And you know, after a few hundred years it's gotten kind of annoying. A noble, proud, strong people chopping away at their own legs. Until now, it's been these Pigment Denied People—we also call them that—doing their best to weaken Native people by targeting the youth. Now it seems Native youth are targeting themselves. There comes a time when even toy robots have to stand up and say, 'This has just got to stop.'"

Everything that could make a sound in the room made a sound. It was a cacophony of agreement from a variety of inanimate objects, though as the boy had found out, "inanimate" was no longer the correct word for things in the Indigenous world.

Once at the top of the food and technology chain, the boy now realized he was definitely at the bottom of the power paradigm that currently existed in his bedroom. In fact, he was finding it difficult to argue his position. How often does a teenager get asked to validate his choice to decrease, however minimally, the Aboriginal population of his community and of Canada? No defence, no rationalization, no justification miraculously sprang to the boy's lips. So, he said nothing.

But the robot would have none of that. It was talking, and it wanted to be talked to. "So, you gonna say anything or stand there like a bump on a log? Which by the way is a stupid saying 'cause most of the log bumps I know are quite opinionated."

The boy opened his mouth, then closed it again.

"Come on. Anything this monumental in your life must have taken loads and loads of consideration. Serious and deep thought. Share with us your rationale."

The whole room seemed to pause, as if waiting for the boy to say something. Anything. His mouth opened, though the brain controlling it wasn't quite sure what was going to be said. But the boy had faith something wise and logical would come out.

"It's hard."

The head on the robot twirled around three times. "'It's hard!' What kind of rationale is—"

"Shut up." For the first time the boy forcibly interjected, cutting off the robot's criticism. "You just... you just shut up. You don't know anything." The boy had taken control, leaving the animated animatronic silent. The whole room looked on in expectation. "Yeah, so you've been around since forever. Big deal. That doesn't mean you know what it's like to be me or understand what I've gone through. Just because you can talk to laptops and log bumps doesn't give you the right to tell me what I should or shouldn't do with my life!"

"Excuse me! Show a little respect here. Do I have to remind you your people worship my people?"

Now the boy had found his rhythm. He'd found his voice, or perhaps his voice had found him. "No they—we—don't. We respect and honour the spirits. Not worship. Because we're all equal, not better or worse."

Just a year ago, the boy had attended a family potlatch and had spent an afternoon listening to one of the village elders talk about this. At the time, the whole topic had seemed kind of silly and he had quickly become bored, not expecting the content of the elder's stories to eventually become so pertinent.

"Dammit…" muttered Mr. Gizmo. He had hoped the boy wouldn't know that. It's a little-known fact that plastic robots hate being one-upped.

"My parents are gone. My grandmother just died. I love my grandfather, but he's passed out in the other room. I don't really belong here, and because of that, I don't have any real friends. I don't fit in, and I don't know what to do." The boy took a breath. "I feel so… alone."

Nothing in the room responded. You could have heard a pin drop, but none of the pins in the room felt like dropping at that specific moment.

The floodgates had been opened, and the boy unleashed a torrent. "It's just… Why? That's all. Why? Why don't I fit in? Why am I here? Why should I continue to put up with this shit? It's all so hard. I am not doing anybody any good, especially me. So there. There's your stupid reason. Happy?!"

Again, the room was silent. Even the old-fashioned clock on the wall seemed reluctant to shatter the quiet with a tick. Finally, the robot's eyes dimmed briefly, then resumed glowing.

"You realize you are talking about the misery of existence to a cheap plastic robot that you've ignored for most of your teenage years. I know about being alone. Look, my left leg has a hairline crack along the back. Two of my lights are burned out. I've got dirt and sand inside most of my working parts. This damp weather is hell on my electronics. Your dog peed on me once, and I can't remember the last time you changed my batteries. Right now, I am operating on sheer willpower."

"So am I," retorted the boy.

"Fair enough," responded the toy. "I don't argue that things may be difficult at the moment. Everything you are feeling… Well, that is what you feel and who the hell am I to tell you not to feel that way? Remember your Uncle Todd?"

Of course he did. Uncle Todd was a legend. Out hunting three Februarys ago, he had gotten lost in a sudden snowstorm and spent eight days surviving on his own until a search party found him holed up in a desolate hunting cabin about six kilometres from where he'd gone missing.

"I know for a fact he was just as down as you are, maybe more, thinking he was lost, that eventually he was going to freeze to death, or maybe slowly starve, or maybe even be eaten by a grizzly bear. More importantly—and this was what ate away at him—he was embarrassed, even humiliated, that he, a good and knowledgeable Kwakwaka'wakw man, had gotten lost in the woods and that right at that moment, people were searching and worrying about him. Each night, as the darkness grew in that dingy cabin, it grew inside him. He'd look over to where his rifle stood and wonder what was the best course of action."

This was definitely news to the boy. His uncle had always seemed so strong and... well, fearless. That he would even consider something like that... For the second time that day, the teenager was surprised.

"But things got better for him. They usually do. Eternity has taught me that. Yes, yes, I know the argument that the world is so depressing and gloomy, so it would just be better to end it all and revel blissfully in non-existence. But the thing is—and keep in mind this is coming from someone who has seen the mountains rise and fall, and then rise again—that is such a narrow perspective on how the world runs. Nothing ends. Everything goes on, and on and on. Taking your own life because life is painful, that doesn't end it. More often than not, that spreads the pain. One person, then another, probably another will see what you've done. Some might follow. Or it might be just your family, sitting there at your funeral, crying, blaming themselves. Suicide becomes a virus, spreading across the youth of a community. And it spreads sadness to everyone. We've all seen it."

The robot was speaking the truth. As horrible as things were for him, the boy definitely did not want to be responsible for other people following his example.

"Is this a..." Once again, the boy searched for the words. "A suicide intervention?"

"No, it's a cultural intervention. You and your generation are the elders of tomorrow. The virus starts and stops with you. I—all of us—happen to like the Kwakwaka'wakw nation and would like to see it survive. We'd like all the First Nations of Canada, the world—what the hell, everybody—to survive. Every once in a while, everybody needs help. Think of this as... I guess you could call it 'spiritual welfare.' We're there when you need us."

The boy was silent. The room was silent. Finally, he asked an important question: "Will things get better?"

The toy's eyes flickered. "I don't know. We're spirits, not fortune tellers. Usually, that's up to you. Other people can knock you down, but only you can get back up. If you don't get back up, if you go to sleep and don't wake up the next morning, they—whoever they are—have won. And everything you and your people believe is important gets a little weaker."

Down the hall, the boy could hear his grandfather wake up. The bed creaked, and footsteps headed for the bathroom. The living room was littered with beer bottles for the first time the boy could remember. A moment of weakness for the old man, who had always seemed so strong. But now the man who had raised him, the man who had just lost the woman he had loved and lived with for forty-seven years, was walking forward. No doubt sadder than the boy could imagine, but carrying on. He had gotten back up.

"What should I do, then?"

Nothing. The toy robot sat on the shelf, staring off into the distance. No lights, no voice, silent as it had been for years.

"Hello? You still in there?"

He picked up the plastic creation and shook it. Around the room the boy could see the objects that just a few minutes ago had shaken his world. They were all silent. Still grasping the toy, he turned the lamp on and off. Flipped through the pages of his graphic novel. Turned the radio on briefly. All seemed perfectly normal... whatever that meant.

Mr. Gizmo's red plastic eyes remained blank, as they had been for as long as the boy could remember. He wiped the dust from the shelf and returned the toy to its former position. After a moment of thought, he grabbed the gun. This time it felt ominous and uncomfortable in his hand. He hoped he could get it back to the old man's closet before his grandfather came out of the bathroom. As he turned toward the door, he felt the gun move slightly. The hammer slowly uncocked and went back to its normal position. And along the side of the revolver, he saw the safety shift to on.

This time, his door opened with no fuss. The boy quickly entered his grandparents' bedroom, then the closet, hastily replacing the gun.

He returned to his room and sat on his bed, trying to fathom the afternoon's events.

Looking up toward the thing on the shelf, he said, "You're never going to talk to me again, are you?"

There was no response, not that he was expecting one. Outside his door, he heard his grandfather return to his room.

Nothing had really changed in the boy's life. Yet so much was different. Tired, that was how he felt. That he could deal with. Getting comfortable on his bed, he hugged his pillow, wondering if there was indeed a spirit inside the fluffy collection of foam. He realized he had to go to the bathroom.

Opening the bathroom door, the first thing the boy saw was the porcelain toilet. As Mr. Gizmo had pointed out, and if thousands of years of Kwakwaka'wakw teaching were true, the toilet had some kind of spirit too. And quite probably it was watching him at this very moment, and all moments.

Suddenly, the boy wasn't sure he had to go anymore.

PETROPATHS

I guess you could say Duane Crow was a bad boy. Everybody knows he'd been in some trouble before. If you were keeping track, you could say a lot of trouble over the years. Never made it past Grade 10. Never held down a job for more than a year; going in and out of jail kind of limits your employment opportunities. Still, I knew he was a good boy. He just made a lot of bad choices. Who hasn't? A lot of you are thinking I have to say that. I'm his grandfather, and I'm giving the eulogy. But I truly believe the boy had untapped potential. And in the end, he proved it to me.

I still remember him as a gap-toothed young boy, climbing trees and swimming in Otter Lake. He loved to explore. He had the whole world before him, and I always thought he was meant for something special. My daughter tried as best she could. His father... Well, the less said about him the better, I suppose. The only good thing he ever did for the boy was teach him how to play guitar. But when Duane's mother passed on seven years ago, I think that was what really derailed him. It was like Duane became angry at the world. He stopped trying… Or I guess you could say he started trying the wrong things. All that unfocused energy got him in so much trouble. Drinking, drugs, fights and, finally, a fondness for taking other people's cars. Only twenty-six years old, and already people had painted him bad for life. That's how he ended up on Thunderbird Island. Thank the Creator for sentencing circles.

White people, feeling so guilty for everything they've done to us over the last five hundred years, are always trying to make amends in one way or another. This year, it was the imposition of a sentencing circle for Native young offenders. The Crown suggested that for lesser crimes the local elders get together and come up with an alternative punishment. As most of you know, the Native way is to repair the damage and heal the wound, not to exact punishment for something already done.

One month on one of our islands, learning the ways of our people, trying to ground himself in tradition. I know Duane didn't really believe in our traditional ways, but maybe he thought this option was a lot easier than half a year of cement, steel and guards at the local jail. Maybe he felt it would be like going camping for a couple weeks. He could be short-sighted that way. Whatever the reason, the important thing was we got him to the island.

I remember when he was brought before the elders after his last little escapade. Afterwards, as I walked him out of the building, he didn't look up. Like I said, inside he was a good boy. Duane knew he'd done bad and was embarrassed to be paraded in front of us all.

"I'm sorry, Poppa. I really am," he said. That's what he called me, Poppa. And I could tell he was speaking the truth. "I don't know why I took that car. I knew I'd get caught."

"When you take these cars, are you running away from something or to something?"

"I… I wanna go someplace, but I don't know where. Other than you, Poppa, this place has been shitty to me. I'm bored. I'm frustrated. I'm… something."

He sounded like a lot of the youth in our community, stuck between the past and the future. The true goal is finding enough of both to make your life worth living.

I told him it was okay, that he was there to make amends for stealing those cars.

"Don't worry," he said. "Someday I'll make you proud. I'll be famous and you'll be able to say with pride, 'That's my grandson.' I promise."

I told him he didn't have to promise me anything. Famous don't mean nothing. I told him just to look after himself and the important things in his life. I told him that's why people often fall off the road into the ditch. That's 90 percent of just getting through the day—looking after things.

Duane nodded before we entered the room where the elders were waiting. "I'll try, Poppa," he said.

We elders felt that Duane's problem was a lack of understanding of his place in the universe. Yeah, I know, that sounds so airy-fairy, like we'd be having him do yoga or something, but it's true. We explained to him that he needed to know who he was, where he came from and what his path was. You can't know where you're going until you know where you've come from. That was one of the things my grandson had to look after. Otherwise, he'd be like a shiny metal ball in one of those pinball machines, just banging here and there, making a lot of noise but not really accomplishing much. I told him I would come over to the island frequently, to give him instruction in the traditions of our people. Still, I don't know if he fully understood what we expected of him.

We chose Thunderbird Island because it's fairly isolated and large enough to provide the boy with some space to wander about and not feel trapped. More importantly, that's where the petroglyphs are. A thousand years or so ago, some of our people carved images on the wall of a cliff, just a dozen feet up from the shore. Overall there seems to be maybe thirty or thirty-five separate images scattered across the limestone wall, ranging in size from the width of a hand to the size of a Hula Hoop. It's difficult to tell what some of the images are supposed to represent. Over the centuries, some have faded, others you aren't sure where one picture stops and another begins, and a few, around the edges, have crumbled off and fallen to the ground. Time and weather can be formidable enemies of Aboriginal art. Not to mention the bunch of carved initials and rude words that populated the edge of the petroglyphs. Reminders left by dozens of stupid people trying to find immortality by hacking away at a sacred site.

This has been a sacred place to us for as long as we can remember. When I was young, I would canoe for hours across the big lake to get there and sit for days, looking at them, trying to figure them out. Some were easily identifiable, like fish and animals. Others were a little more unusual. A few were just bizarre. Sprinkled among them were non-specific shapes that some anthropologist once described as geometric. As a kid, I just thought they were pretty.

It took me a while to understand these were the musings and dreams of our ancestors, the thoughts and history of our people carved into Mother Earth for us to see. People always told me I was just imagining it, but I was sure I could feel a delicate hum coming from those rocks. A subtle vibration. Nobody else felt it, so I always figured they were right and it was my own silliness. As I learned later, I wasn't alone in my silliness.

We felt that putting Duane so close to the petroglyphs, literally on their doorstep, would be like the heart and soul of his people looking over his shoulder, giving him a path to follow. Being on Thunderbird Island would give him some time to look after things. Sometimes being alone with yourself, with your thoughts and realizations, can be more trying than a long prison term. Or for some, it can teach you a lot more than one of those degrees at a university. It depends on the person. I hoped Duane would do as I had done and ponder the images so lovingly etched into the rock. Long hours in front of them had taught me patience and contemplation. But Duane seemed more interested in making sure he had enough cigarettes to get him through the week, till I would show up with his next boatful of supplies.

We arrived at Thunderbird Island and unloaded the boat. "So, what am I supposed to do until you get back?" Duane asked me.

I told him, "Wake up with the sun. Go to bed with the sun. Make yourself some tea. Look at those pictures on the wall. Respect life."

"That's it?!"

I think he was expecting more, like it was some sort of boot camp.

"Yep, that's it. The only thing I, or anybody, can really teach you is to do what you can to be a good person. I know that probably sounds stupid, but the only reason we're put on this earth, I believe, is to try and make it a better place when we leave than when we entered it. See, that's the real trick. Everything else is just details."

His forehead crinkled as he processed what I had said. Next, I filled him in on the rules: he was not to leave the island for any reason. Everything he needed, outside of the food I would bring, was on that island. It was up to him to figure out what he needed in this world. That was his responsibility—to figure things out. Why he was so angry. What he needed in life to be happy. Why he took things. Why he fought people. Why he had ended up there on Thunderbird Island. He had to look after things.

I left him there that first week, a gradually diminishing figure on a Central Ontario beach, looking confused and a little apprehensive. I don't think he'd ever spent a week by himself, alone, with no way of talking to other people or occupying his time. Duane always acted tough, but as my boat pulled away I thought I saw that little boy I remembered, so confused and hurt, asking me where his father was.

So he spent that first week alone on Thunderbird Island. Later, he told me he just about went crazy with boredom. Basically, getting firewood, swatting mosquitos and swimming were the only things to do. So he would sit there where he had set up camp, watching the birds, occasionally strumming his guitar. After some discussion, we elders had decided to allow him to bring the guitar. It wasn't like we were sending him to one of those Russian prisons or anything. By the end of the second day, he had named all the birds that liked to hang around his camp. Same with the chipmunks and squirrels and a porcupine that watched him from a nearby tree during the day, always changing trees at night.

It was on the third day that he found himself in front of the petroglyphs. He'd seen them a couple times as a kid, when his family or the school would bring him out for a day trip. But this time, with a good fifteen hours of June daylight to kill, he propped up his lawn chair directly in front of the wall. Normally, doing exactly what he'd been told to do would have grated on Duane's pride, but he had pretty much exhausted all the other time-wasting possibilities on the island.

So he sat there, playing his guitar, smoking and looking at the images. He told me he would string some of the images together and make up stories to pass the hours. Two days of this. By the third day, he found himself letting those carved images just wash over him, like an aroma or light. That day he barely touched his guitar. Instead, he would lean forward, frequently leaving his chair, and approach the engraved hollows. His fingers touched them, feeling their texture and tracing the images chiselled into the soft limestone. Like there was a message somewhere in the ageless stone. All those stories he had been making up about the carvings started falling to the ground. A different saga was emerging from the weathered rock.

When I returned that Sunday, I saw him standing on the shallow beach, waiting. Again I saw the little boy he'd once been, so lonely yet happy at my arrival.

"There you are. I wasn't sure you were coming!" was his greeting to me.
"I ain't got no place else to be. Besides, I thought you might be hungry."
I brought out a bucket of fried chicken, his favourite as a kid. I guess he was still a kid deep inside, because he grabbed it right out of my hand and ripped into it. His only other comment, between drumsticks, was "You bring my cigarettes?"

After unloading the boat, I spent a couple hours catching up with him. The day was mostly consumed with me doing my elder thing and telling him what he should do now that he was comfortable on the island. We talked a while about ceremonies and teachings. I gave him some sage and sweet grass. He seemed receptive, almost interested.

I spoke of nature, of the Creator, of the importance of having respect for other people and, just as important, respect for yourself. Normally Duane would have rolled his eyes at this lecture, but I guess he was so starved for the sound of a human voice that he listened. Didn't ask many questions, just listened, till near the end.

All around I could hear the birds scolding us for disturbing their little island. Off in the distance, a Sea-Doo was making a racket as it crossed the lake some miles away. I could tell he was biding his time to ask me something. Finally, he worked up the nerve.

"Those petroglyphs... they're something special, aren't they? I mean, I thought they were just pretty things chipped into a wall. But there's a purpose to them, ain't there?"

I asked why he thought that.

"Just a feeling."

"What kind of feeling?" I pressed.

A moment passed, then the old Duane came back, because the only answer I got was a shrug.

When I returned the subsequent week, I could tell the carvings were beginning to consume his interest. As soon as I got out of the boat, he ushered me toward the wall. He had moved his camp to directly in front of it, and there was a pile of cigarette butts scattered across the pine needles there. I asked if he'd been doing the ceremonies I had taught him, but I don't think he heard me. Duane put his hand on one of the carvings, the one that looked like a turtle.

"Put your hand here. Tell me if you feel anything."

He grabbed my hand and held it up against the wall, looking at me with an odd intensity. I felt the rough texture of the limestone, the softness of some moss, the shallow indent of what had been laboriously carved into the sedimentary rock thousands of years ago. Then I remembered my own youth. The humming. But putting my hand on that rock wall, I didn't feel anything.

"You're talking about the buzzing, aren't you?" I asked.

He smiled, glad I knew what he was talking about. "Not buzzing. It's not totally something you hear. And it's not vibrating, something you can just feel. It's a combination of both. Or neither. Or something else completely. It's so slight and elusive… I wasn't sure it was even there. But you know what I'm talking about. I'm not crazy."

That's what he said to me that day. Once more I listened to the rock with my hand, but what I had experienced in my younger years was no longer there.

Instead, I told my grandson of my own experiences with those petroglyphs. But I had had children coming and a life to live. I had obligations. Several members of my family had pointed out to me that I had spent way too much time on this stupid island with nothing to show for it. My grandson was glad to find out he wasn't crazy. I was pretty happy to find out I wasn't either.

"Wonder what it is," he said.

"Maybe it's an underground river or something," I suggested, not very convincingly.

As we ate our lunch, his attention kept returning to the wall of images. After some prodding, Duane shared with me more of his thoughts regarding those petroglyphs. It seemed my wayward and unfocused grandson had been studying them pretty deeply. He'd noticed that they were arranged in some sort of pattern. He wasn't sure what the pattern was or meant, but he said if you sat there long enough and let the glyphs tell you their own story their own way, you could almost make it out, like a whisper in the wind. Those were his words. He said you couldn't help but notice after a while that there was a sort of order to all the things carved into that wall. Like it was the Earth telling us a story, he said. Or more accurately, he added, like it was a song waiting to be sung.

"What if," he said, his voice cracking with growing excitement, "the petroglyphs are like that set of lines musicians write, and each of the images is a note?"

Duane pulled out his guitar and played me a couple bars of music. And then he played them again, with the odd wrong note inserted where a right note had been. The song didn't work. The magic was lost. That's what the wall reminded him of—a pattern of pictures. Some of the carvings had been added over the years, but the wrong image in the wrong place. But a lot of them were in the right place. He thought that's what was causing the buzzing or humming or whatever it was.

By this time, I was thinking that maybe we had been wrong to put Duane on this island alone for the last two weeks. It was true I hadn't seen him so flushed with excitement or focused on something positive in a long time. I mean, it was good that he had developed a connection with what his ancestors had done a long time ago, but I was beginning to get a little worried. I remember saying to my grandson that maybe it was time he came back to the mainland, that he'd spent enough time on Thunderbird Island. He looked at me like I had asked him to fly to the moon.

"No thanks, Poppa. I'm not done yet."

I wasn't sure if he was talking about his court-mandated sentence or something else. Anyway, I had inadvertently closed the door on the topic and we'd reached the end of our conversation. Duane didn't want to talk anymore, about the petroglyphs or anything else. The wall he had spent years building, emotional brick by emotional brick, had once again risen into place. So, still a little worried, I packed up my boat and returned across the lake to the mainland, concerned about what my next trip to the island might bring. Behind me I could see him on the shore, watching my motorboat plow through the water. Then I saw him turn and walk toward the petroglyphs.

That next week was the longest of my life. I kept telling myself there was nothing to worry about. The Creator had indeed made a complex and mysterious world, but most of it was explainable. I left at dawn the following Sunday, needing to make sure my grandson was okay, a little afraid of what I might find.

After two hours in my motorboat navigating the submerged tree stumps and rocky outcroppings common in the Canadian Shield lakes, I saw him waiting for me on the landing spit. I felt better. All his camping equipment was packed, and he looked calm and ready to return to the world of the reserve. In fact, he looked more than ready. There was a sense of excitement about him and an eagerness to move forward, but he was unwilling to talk about it much. He just said everything was okay, he just needed to check some things out.

"Like what?" I asked.

"I'll let you know when I know" was all he said.

As he settled into the front of the boat, I saw something sticking out of his backpack. It had feathers.

"What's that?" I asked.

He looked at it for a moment before pulling it out and handing it to me. It looked like a tomahawk. Not one you'd find at the local craft store, made for three bucks but costing the tourists fifteen. It looked real. We hadn't made real tomahawks on the Otter Lake First Nation in almost two hundred years. Still, the binding was leather and sinew, holding the oval stone in place, making it a truly dangerous weapon. Dyed porcupine quills gave colour and texture to the foot-and-a-half-long handle. To these old eyes, it was an impressive piece of work.

"Where'd you get this?"

Shrugging, he looked back at the island. "I found it."

That was kind of hard to believe. It didn't appear to have been weathered by several hundred years of exposure to the elements, and if I hadn't known better, the front of the stone looked stained with what looked like blood. Things weren't adding up, I thought.

"Where'd you find it?"

He pointed back at the island. "Over there."

"On the island?"

"Yep."

"Where on the island?"

It was a moment before he answered my question. "I don't know yet."

That was the last thing Duane said on our trip. He tucked the tomahawk back into his bag. The attitude that had originally gotten him into trouble and sent to the island had been transformed. The look of anger or rebellion was replaced with contemplation and interest. His mind seemed wrapped around a thought. The moment my boat hit the dock, he thanked me quickly and trotted off down the road. Something had happened to my grandson, and I didn't know what.

A few days passed and something about the way Duane had acted kept eating away at me. All this talk about the petroglyphs, the tomahawk and the changed attitude made me think the path we had chosen for this young man was changing direction. Duane had been living with his father's sister since his return from the island, and she told me over the phone that he seemed to be staying out of trouble, spending a lot of time on the internet, looking at all sorts of strange stuff. Other than video games and porn, he'd never had much time for doing anything on that computerized thing. But now he was on it late into the night, focused and eager, like a young buck on his first moose hunt.

So I decided to pay my grandson a visit. When I arrived he was on the computer, tucked away in the corner of the living room. On top of the monitor was that tomahawk. As I approached, I could see the screen. He was looking at rocks. Much bigger than the ones on the island. Tall ones standing in a circle. Maybe he was interested in a career in geology, I tried to tell myself. Duane didn't look up when I approached. It was like there was a tunnel connecting his eyes to the screen. I'd seen a similar look in strip clubs, back in my youth.

"Hey, Grandson, find anything interesting on that thing?"

Duane looked over his shoulder at the sound of my voice, gave me a quick smile and nod, then just as quickly went back to looking at the screen. I tried to coax him out a bit, talk to him as I had when he was young, but he had no time for me. He wasn't rude about it, just severely preoccupied. I decided to play his game.

"So, what's so damn interesting about those big rocks? More interesting than your own grandfather?"

I could see the question registering, and luckily for me, it opened him up.

"It's a place called Stonehenge, Poppa. In England. It's thousands and thousands of years old. They're not exactly sure what it was used for, but they think it might be a calendar of some kind."

It looked awfully big and awkward to be a calendar—I kept a much smaller one in my wallet—but I kept my mouth shut. About that, anyway.

"Okay, so it's a big stone calendar. That's interesting to you? Those English people are weird anyway. Do you know they drink their beer warm?"

No response to my joke. His fingers started hunting and pecking across the keyboard, making a clicking sound. Other images popped up pretty quick.

"These are the Nazca Lines, somewhere down in Peru. Kilometres and kilometres of pictures scratched into the ground by Native people a long time ago."

The images my grandson showed me looked kind of pretty, I thought, pictures of spiders and hummingbirds etched in the dirt. Why somebody would want to do that I couldn't figure out, but it certainly looked nice.

"Again, scientists have all sorts of ideas about what they could be, but nothing definite. And look at this…" Once again, his fingers clicked and clacked on those plastic buttons. More images came up. "These are rock carvings in Scotland. Five thousand years old." I heard the computer go click again. "And these etchings in a boulder were found in Egypt. They're from long before they built those pyramids and stuff. Like 4000 BC or something." Click. "This is Machu Picchu, a mysterious Incan city made almost entirely out of rock." Another click and a wall of different yet familiar images appeared. "This is called Judaculla Rock, in North Carolina. Doesn't it look a lot like the petroglyphs on Thunderbird Island?"

It did indeed. I was beginning to notice a theme.

"A lot of people in this world do interesting things with rocks, I suppose."

He nodded, almost too eagerly. "Yeah, but I've been reading up on these things. There are articles and pictures all over the internet about this kind of grid configuration. If you mark all the places that have petroglyphs, or places where rocks are used in sacred ways, on a map of the Earth, they look like a network, or graph maybe. Definitely there's a pattern of some sort to them."

Now, even I knew that the internet was a place you could find theories about everything—that Elvis was still alive, that one race of people actually ruled the world (which would be a huge surprise to our chief and band council), that aliens were responsible for the success of McDonald's. The internet breeds conspiracy theories like the swamp behind my house breeds mosquitos. I tried to tell him that, but he wasn't listening.

"Why are you so fixated on this?" I asked my grandson.

For a moment, I saw him pause. Then his eyes darted back to the computer screen, and I could see he was trying to make a decision.

"It's kinda hard to explain."

"Have you tried?"

I could tell something was fighting in his head.

"I'll tell you tomorrow," he offered. "Why don't you come for dinner? Aunt Maggie will be at work, but she usually leaves me a casserole or something."

I agreed.

We made some small talk, but the conversation had ended. As I left the house, I wondered what he was up to. All this mystery. Was he back to doing bad things again? I didn't think so. Bad things and research about rocks and petroglyphs seldom went together. I decided to do a bit of research of my own. Not on a computer, but in the real world.

The next morning, I was on my way to Thunderbird Island. A man of my age doesn't do overnight trips to rocky islands much, so I opted to spend as much of the day there as possible. The sun was barely up as I pulled away from the dock. A few hours later, as I approached the island, I saw another boat pulled up on the shore. It took me a few minutes before I recognized it as Maggie's boat. Duane must have borrowed it to come back over. But I could tell the campsite, petroglyphs and, I got the feeling, the whole island were deserted. Duane knew better than to abandon his aunt's boat. And since it was an island, where would he go without that boat? More mystery, and a man my age doesn't take well to mysteries. It's way too much effort to figure them out.

As mysteries go, the first clue was easy to find. It was located on the petroglyph wall. Two new carvings. The limestone chips and dust were lying fresh on the moss at the base. About three feet up, maybe seven inches long, was a stick figure wearing what looked like a baseball cap. Duane. Maybe six feet farther up was a spiral, similar to one Duane had shown me the day before on his computer, in one of those far-off places. He had defaced this sacred site. I was angry. I was really angry. Not only was this illegal by white men's laws, it was deeply disrespectful by our own beliefs. I planned to have a very serious and possibly loud word or two with that boy. Elders aren't supposed to yell, but I felt this time it was due.

Not knowing what else to do—contrary to what you may have heard, elders aren't all-knowing—I decided to go home and maybe cool down. I was half tempted to tow Maggie's boat back and leave the boy stranded, but then I thought, Screw it. He took it out here and abandoned it, let him deal with her wrath. I was done doing favours for that boy. He was on his own.

The sun was just about to dip beneath the treeline when I heard footsteps coming up my driveway. I was enjoying my afternoon tea, so it took me a moment to recognize the step pattern—that's something us old geezers can do. Some of us know the sound of how every person in the village walks. It's like how people speak; no two people have the same footsteps. It was Duane, back from whatever mischief he'd been up to. I'd been thinking all day about what I was going to say to him. Should I yell at him for an hour and then kill him, or kill him and then yell at him? I'm exaggerating of course, but sometimes kids and grandkids will make you feel that way. Regardless, I figured I'd feel the situation out before making a decision.

Before he got to the door, I yelled to him, "I know it's you, Duane. You get your ass in here." I stood to meet him as the screen door opened.

What walked through that door startled me. Yesterday, Duane had been clean-shaven, washed and maintained. This Duane had a three-or-four-day beard growth. His hair looked like it hadn't been washed in a week. And even from clear across the living room, I could smell his BO. It was the kind that had fermented over several days and naturally kept the mosquitos away.

"Where the hell have you been?"

"I know we were gonna have dinner at Maggie's tonight... It was tonight, wasn't it? But I thought maybe I should come over here first. Hope that's okay?" I noticed he had his backpack with him when he dropped it to the ground with a loud and heavy thud. "I know you got a lot of questions..."

"Damn right I do! What the hell have you been up to and—"

"Sorry, Poppa, but you got anything to eat? I haven't eaten a lot in the last few days. I have to remember to bring more food."

I didn't really know what he meant, but he was my grandson, and hospitality has been part of our culture since Time Immemorial, even when it comes to rude, crazy grandkids. Two sandwiches and a carton of milk later, he asked to take a shower. It was almost half an hour before he finally sat down at the table with me, wearing a pair of my track pants and a spare T-shirt I am ashamed to say has grown a little small for me.

"What's wrong with the shower at Maggie's? And she doesn't feed you either?"

Duane smiled like these were the questions of a child. We elders don't get a lot of smiles like that, and it made me kind of mad.

"Well?"

He opened his backpack and removed something long and thin, then hid it under the tablecloth. "I got something to show you first," he said, "and it's part of the answer to your question."

My grandson then placed it on the table in front of me. It looked like one of those old-time flintlock pistols, like in those pirate movies or something. I picked it up. It was heavy and smelled of what I assumed was gunpowder.

"Did you steal this?" I asked.

A sequence of expressions flashed across his face: surprise, a little shame and then amusement.

"I know what you're thinking. You're right. I did steal it. But not from a store." From here, to put it politely, his story got a bit weird. In fact, I struggled to make sense of it. "I took it off what I think was a coureur de bois. At least, that's what we were told to call them in school. I'm going to have to research them, but you know, those French guys who traded goods for furs with Native people a long time ago. That's who I took it from. That's where I've been. Oh, Poppa, it's great to be back."

"You took it from somebody that hasn't prowled these woods in hundreds of years? And just how did you do this?"

Duane started flossing his teeth. I guess there was no floss back in coureur de bois times.

"You know, for people who spent all their time travelling this wild country, living off the land, battling rapids and all sorts of difficulties, you'd think they'd be a lot braver than they actually were. I also brought back some axes and beaver pelts that I left on the island. I'm kind of new to this, Poppa, and I need some advice. I'd like to start paying rent at Aunt Maggie's and was thinking about selling them to a museum or something, but I wanted to clear it with you. I didn't want you to think I was doing bad things again."

Here came the big question. "You brought them back from where?"

He smiled again, before taking a deep breath. "Well, here's where it gets complicated. I don't know if it was a different dimension, or maybe a universe with the same kind of history, or maybe I just travelled back in time. I haven't figured that out yet. I should have paid more attention in science class back in school, but I know it's something like that. It has to be. Got any potato chips? That's what I've been craving for the last three days."

"You were back in time... or in another... What did you call it... dimension? For the last three days?!"

"Yeah, it took longer than I thought. I lost my hammer and chisel when I fell in the river. You know Otter Lake used to be an actual river way back when? A fast-moving one, too. I guess that's why the coureurs de bois were using it. I had to steal some stuff from their camp to survive. It's amazing what you can do with a flashlight and a cellphone that plays recorded messages. Scared the heck out of them, and they ran off like spooked rabbits. Boy, was I terrified for a moment. But here I am. Salt and vinegar if you have them."

Somehow, as I tried to figure all this out, I got him his chips. Duane seemed quite earnest and sincere. As problematic as he had been as a child, then later as an adult, was he really the type to sit there and lie directly to my face? Or worse than that, maybe he thought I was a complete idiot. The final possibility was my grandson was crazy. None of these options were particularly appealing.

It seemed Duane could tell by the expression on my face that I was having a little trouble believing his story.

"I guess I wouldn't believe it either. But I swear to you, Poppa, that's where I was. And it has to do with those petroglyphs."

Whether or not I believed him, I had figured out it had something to do with that place.

"The two new carvings on the wall... that was you?"

"Yep, that's how it works. Except there's four there now."

Okay, now I knew the boy was lying. "No, I was there this morning. I saw the two new carvings... Only two."

"Yeah, those were what—I guess you could say—opened the door and let me... 'travel' is the best word I can use. I had to add a note to the song of the petroglyphs, one that matched the rhythm of the other ones that were already there."

"What the hell are you talking about?"

"And of course, I had to carve another to get back. You probably didn't notice the one I'd carved a few days ago to get back with the tomahawk because it had aged over the years and looked like the rest. If you look closely, you'll notice another new one I just added a couple hours ago... or centuries ago, depending on how you want to look at it."

Something suddenly occurred to him, making him look at me with new interest. "Or maybe you won't. I mean, for you, they will have always been there, so maybe that's why you didn't notice the first one. This all gets so complicated. Time, or dimension, travel isn't for the stupid, I guess."

By now I was wondering if I should call 911.

"Back when I was on the island, I could tell those pictures weren't random or haphazard. There was a story or pattern there. I told you that. It took a while, but I've figured out the pattern of the glyphs. It was kind of like a code, so I think now I know how to use them. I've been through them twice. You add to it, and it... like... increases whatever power is there and opens some sort of door. It's so cool."

I remembered the music analogy he'd explained to me by playing his guitar and thought there was a weird sort of logic to what he was saying. Over the years, a lot of idiots had carved their initials into the limestone surrounding the ancient pictures, but probably no mysterious time door-ways opened up for them.

"And then I got back to the mainland and read about all those places around the world. They're all connected somehow. One guy says it's because of the resonant harmonics in the crystals located in the igneous rocks. It creates a sort of frequency that somehow manages to open these doors." This did not sound like my car-stealing grandson at all. "These places of power occur at regular intervals around the world. It's like our ancestors knew and understood this, that's why they put the petroglyphs there. But over the years, we forgot about them. I guess we were too busy dealing with all the white men who had suddenly appeared. Then smallpox and measles probably killed off a lot of wise people. But I figured it out, Poppa, I could see what they had done. I'm not as stupid as everybody thinks I am."

I wanted to tell my grandson that nobody thought he was stupid, but I didn't get the chance.

"I told you that I would make you proud of me. I'll be famous for more than stealing cars. Everybody will know me and Otter Lake. I've done what nobody else—at least in a long time—has been able to do. All by myself. Just think of all the things we can accomplish, the history we can change. It's amazing, the possibilities. Maybe I'll go back and kick Columbus's and Custer's asses!" Duane laughed at his own joke. "History isn't in books anymore. We can walk through it."

Once again I saw that young boy I'd loved since long ago, wanting to be appreciated and applauded, like all children.

I was beginning to put two and two together, at least within the context of what Duane was trying to tell me. Whether I believed every single word my grandson told me was another matter.

"That tomahawk you showed me a couple days ago. That's where you got it... through the petroglyphs?"

"Yep. I think it was our ancestors'. How far back, I don't know. I know there's some way to tell by looking at the stars and mapping the constel-lations, and then comparing them with the way they look today, but I'll figure that out later. Hey, but one guy I saw paddling a canoe looked a lot like Uncle Floyd."

As any grandfather and elder worth his salt knows, the power in a good story shouldn't be dismissed. However, all this talk of time travel and dimension-hopping was getting way over my head.

"So this is what you're doing with your life now? Travelling through time and dimensions, stealing stuff?"

For a moment, he looked embarrassed and a little hurt. "No. I got bigger plans. I just wanted to have something to show you—and everybody else—that I wasn't lying." He finished the bag of chips.

I picked up the flintlock gun and had to admit it looked pretty real. I had no idea what a fake one looked like, but if this was bogus, somebody sure had put a lot of time and effort into making a convincingly decent fake.

"You can keep it, Poppa. It's yours."

All this was too much for an old man. I had run out of questions.

"You know how you always talk about how we have to struggle to keep what culture we have, hold on to the language, all that stuff. Now you don't have to worry. Everything our ancestors had, we can have again." His eyes were gleaming with those amazing possibilities he had mentioned.

Admittedly, my experience as an elder hadn't really prepared me for a conversation like this, but I had seen enough science fiction movies to know this kind of thing was dangerous. Those Anishinabe and coureurs de bois that he had run into on those two trips—supposedly run into—were probably tough customers. I told my grandson of my concerns, but he was like a kid with a motorcycle, thinking only of the speed and the thrill, not of the potential accidents.

"I'll be good, Poppa. You'll see. And… and… and I can do so much good. I'll be able to answer so many questions. I'll be able to help our people back then, you know, deal with everything that's going to happen. Maybe sometime you can come back with me." He suddenly got more excited. "Yeah, you can speak Anishinabe way better than me. Let's do it sometime! Okay?"

I had no answer at that time. I wish I had.

Gathering his stuff up, still smiling, he left my house. That was about two weeks ago. I didn't see him for a week. Logic told me that he was in hiding, trying to make me think he'd gone through that doorway of his. Giving more substance to his story. That he was actually up to something he didn't want me to know about, that this was just some big con or something. I do believe there are places in this world, and I guess all the other worlds that may be out there, that ordinary men and women shouldn't walk. They're not meant to. Especially twenty-six-year-old car thieves.

Something kept gnawing at me, and I went over to the island. As I had half expected, I discovered two new images etched into the wall, but no Duane. I found myself placing my hand on the rock. The same place Duane had put my hand just a few weeks ago. It might have been my imagination, but I thought I could feel a buzzing... then I heard a groan.

It was Duane, lying on the far side of his boat, nestled behind some cedar shrubs. He was running a high fever and was barely conscious. A rash of some sort had spread across his face and neck. I could see some on his hands and arms too. Some years earlier, my son had given me one of those cellphones. I rarely used it, but I couldn't think of a better reason. Because of my high blood pressure and diabetes, I had the health clinic's number programmed in. It was ringing when Duane grabbed my arm, surprisingly strong for somebody in his condition.

"I tried to help. I did, Poppa, 'cause I knew you'd want me to. It was horrible. I tried to make the world a better place... but I don't think I should have..."

His eyes rolled back in his head and he threw up what looked like blood, but it was so dark and thick. A good and proper elder shouldn't curse, but I didn't care. As I waited for help to arrive, I found myself growing angrier and angrier—angry at my grandson for his foolishness, angry at myself for bringing him to this island, angry at the island for what it had done to Duane.

Now, I know nothing about this science stuff, and I tended to lean a little more toward the skeptical end of the spectrum, especially when it came to Duane's story. Today, I'm not so rigid in that department. He did get his wish, though. He did become famous... He's been all over the news. I've been interviewed a half-dozen times myself about it all. I kept most of his claims to myself, for obvious reasons. As for his theory about the petroglyphs as a doorway to other times or other dimensions, I am now leaning more toward his time-travel theory.

How else would you explain the fact that he was the first person to die of smallpox in North America since the 1930s? Doctors say the disease was stamped out worldwide in the 1970s. Nobody knows where or how Duane caught it. In fact, it seems downright impossible by medical standards. At the moment, as you know, the whole reserve is under quarantine and we had to get special permission for this funeral. My arm looks like a pincushion from all the blood that's been taken and all the inoculations I've been given.

Most people forget that a couple hundred years ago, a lot of Native people around here died of the disease. Just as, I figure, we've lost the knowledge of how to use the petroglyphs properly. If you toy with them, they will toy with you.

Duane pointed out to me that a lot of these mysterious engravings were done by people now long gone. Strong, vibrant, imaginative people. Did they die out, he wondered to me, get mixed in with other tribes, or did they just slip into the crack between the worlds and end up somewhere else? Now that's an interesting question.

Sometimes, when I'm lying in bed now, I can feel a slight buzzing in my hand. Almost like the petroglyphs are calling me.

STARS

It was the third streak of light he'd seen that night. Those mysterious glimpses of blurred motion arching across the night sky. Lying on either side of him at their summer camp, his father and uncle were deep in their own dreams, but Nimki found the sky to be a much more interesting companion. Although he was only fourteen summers old, he felt like those distant beacons dangling far above him were ancient friends. Even though he was familiar with every pattern and configuration hanging above the trees, Nimki knew precious little else about the stars, just the stories the elders told him. They were lights from the campfires of hunters and fishermen in the next world. Perhaps one of those campfires belonged to his grandfather, who had left his body and this world two winters past. Since then, occasionally Nimki would pick a star randomly and imagine his grandfather huddled over it, licking his lips in anticipation, a fat sky grouse slowly cooking over its flames.

Next to him, his sleeping uncle rolled over onto his side with a grunt. They'd left the village three days ago in search of deer or moose, or anything sizable to feed the village. Summer was supposed to be a time of plenty, but the wildlife didn't seem to know that. Other than the odd raccoon and rabbit, the three mighty Anishinabe hunters had nothing to show for their time in the bush. Nimki's father was getting frustrated. The boy could tell because he was beginning to talk in monosyllables... a dangerous sign. His mother, back in the village, was pregnant and needed good, hearty food to produce a healthy baby. Nimki's father usually fulfilled one of the requirements of manhood by supplying the family and village with tangible supplies but this summer was proving to be a more difficult endeavour. The Creator was making them search long and hard for meat.

Once again, his uncle shifted in his sleep, trying to find a more comfortable position. This was probably the last summer his uncle would be in the village. After many years of searching, he had finally found an excellent woman willing to be his wife. But she lived in another village, several weeks' travel to the east. When the summer ended, he would leave his family... and Nimki... and join this new wife and her community. It was difficult to say whether Nimki or his father would ever see him again. This eventuality was making Nimki's father even more moody. So far on this trip, they had managed to avoid the uncomfortable, looming topic.

He was a good uncle, Nimki thought. It was he more than his father who had taught Nimki the proper way to make a bow and how to shoot it. His father always seemed too busy with Nimki's two brothers and his sister, or doing his duties for the village. Nimki's still-childless uncle, however, seemed to have all the time in the world and Nimki revelled in it. Fortunately, patience was one of his uncle's virtues, for Nimki was not so adept with a bow. Although he spent hours practising, the arrows never seemed to go where he wanted them to. Another point of frustration for the boy's father.

In another time and another place, knowledgeable people would be able to tell that Nimki had been born without a lens in his right eye, severely limiting his depth perception, a requirement for aiming and shooting arrows. Right now and right here, the boy merely thought he was a bad hunter. But what he lacked in ability, he made up for in determination and drive. He was fast becoming one of the best trackers in the village. You didn't need depth perception for that. Usually, it took years of training and experience to track an animal the way Nimki could. He was even better than his uncle and his father. Yet another twinge of embarrassment for his father. But it is difficult to track animals that aren't there. Regardless, that is how all three came to be here, sleeping under the canopy of stars. Except the boy was not sleeping.

Sometimes, Nimki noticed, those fires in the sky seemed to shimmer, almost flicker, the way torches sometimes do when reflected off a wavy pond or lake. And they also seemed to be of slightly different colours and sizes. Some of his ancestors must have bonfires and others just small campfires. What else could that mean?

Other times, staring up into the speckled darkness, he felt if he wished hard enough or maybe opened his mind just right, his body might lift and travel up and up, eventually disappearing amid those shimmering lights. What would he find, he wondered. Such silly thoughts, but still, why was the night sky so much more interesting than the day sky? During the day it was always blue, though occasionally masked by clouds. The sun was there with monotonous regularity, and occasionally the moon would emerge on the opposite side, with bits of it missing. There were all sorts of stories to explain all that existed above and around him. But for Nimki, nighttime was so much more interesting—yes, it was easier to see and do things in the light, but in the absence of the sun, the world above became a more fascinating place.

Pondering such thoughts as he lay nestled on a bed of moss and pine needles, Nimki continued to stare up into the darkness. It was late in the summer, so there were few mosquitos to trouble him. Sometimes his eyes would fixate on an individual beacon of brightness in the dark canopy of the sky. Other times he would unfocus his eyes as best he could and let the whole panorama flood his consciousness. On occasion, he would also wonder, could his grandfather or those other hunters way up there see his campfire? Did they wonder about him and his little fire? Such silly questions.

His family often wondered why he was always tired. It seemed to them that he was only well rested in winter, when the boy's people moved into the warm wigwams, or when it was cloudy and rainy for days. Nimki had difficulty explaining his interest in the night sky. He had tried once to tell his best friend, Keesic, who just shrugged, uninterested in such ideas.

Suddenly, his eyes caught another flash of light streaking through the mottled blackness. A flaming arrow perhaps, from the world above?

A falling torch that burned out before it landed on Turtle Island, maybe? He wished he knew.

Tomorrow, he and the two older men would continue the hunt, and it might be a better day. Just before they'd stopped for the night, they'd discovered some deer droppings. They were a few days old, but it was still a good sign.

Tomorrow night, the sun would set and the moon would rise, as it had ever since he and the elders could remember. With it, the stars would come out again, the same, or maybe slightly different. Some moved occasionally. The sky was a very mysterious place. Nimki wasn't so mysterious. He just loved watching the stars through the trees overhead.

And sometimes, he felt the stars were watching him.

*   *   *

The sound of the door slamming was still echoing across the bay, re- minding Walter how far sound can travel over water. He marched across the lawn—the grass was indeed in need of cutting, as his father had yelled at him repeatedly that night, spitting droplets of beer. His mother, not really paying attention, had changed the channel on the television and turned up the volume. As usual, neither his father nor his mother rushed out the door after him to stall his angry exit, or comfort him and beg him to come back into the house. Other parents, he knew, would have followed such an angry and upset boy out of the house and through the yard, eager to cajole him into returning home with them, maybe held him the way he'd seen other parents do. Possibly even make him some hot chocolate or let him watch what he wanted on television.

Instead, the door and the screen door remained shut. As with much of his life, Walter was alone. He had nowhere to go. He couldn't go to his friend Todd's place. It would be too embarrassing to tell him his parents were drunk and yelling once more. His grandparents were certainly not within walking distance. His options were limited.

So as usual, he found himself at the mound. Sometime in years past, during a construction boom on the reserve, somebody had dumped a sizable pile of earth in a small glen at the edge of their property. A lilac bush hid it from the house. The mound rose about eight feet or so from the ground, the base partially covered by an abundance of weeds. Over the years, the elements, and Walter's body, had flattened the top down to the point where a teenage boy could lie on it.

Even before the boy started climbing up the side, he was breathing heavily. Walter kept telling himself that he wasn't going to cry. Not this time. Not again. Each footstep coming down on the packed earth was another stomp holding down his emotions. With a thump, he sat down at the crest of the hill. It was a dark night, and in the distance he could hear scattered dogs barking. Luckily it hadn't rained in more than a week, so the mound was merely dusty, not muddy. Walter brought his knees up to his chest and wrapped his arms around them, peering out at his sad kingdom: the lilac bush with his parents' house behind it, a disintegrating Chrysler LeBaron parked near the treeline for parts, a school desk for a little kid that had somehow made its way onto this part of the property. Not much of a kingdom. Still, he tried to tell himself, it was better than some had.

Lying back, he took another deep breath. It was Sunday night, and another week of school would begin tomorrow. Only a few hours earlier, Walter had been at church, once again at his mother's command. She'd already given up on her husband, convinced the man was going to hell, but she was determined not to lose her son to ways not of the church. She was going to make sure her progeny knew the power and glory of the Lord, no matter what. The fact that during the rest of the week she paid no mind to the lessons of the Gospel was of little importance to the woman. Sunday night in the pews was her get-out-of-jail-free card. She was probably drunk by now. The darker it got, the higher his parents' blood alcohol level. As reliable as the sun rising.

Unlike many kids, Walter looked forward to school. It got him out of here—for a few hours, anyway. The reserve was a small universe with few places to hide. Tomorrow, science class was first thing in the morning and they were studying astronomy. He liked that class. It provided fun and interesting facts. Anything fun and interesting was a bonus for him. More importantly, the class supplied a much-needed distraction. It was fodder for his imagination. A lot of the other students were bored by the math and science of the topic, but not Walter. He loved the possibilities taught in that class. Just last week, their teacher, Mr. Hughes, had told them about the recent rush to discover habitable planets in the galaxy and how scientists would find them. Evidently, there were two ways to ascertain the existence of hospitable planets: by measuring the wobble of the stars resulting from the gravity of a planet yanking on them, or the minute, almost minuscule dimming of the stars' light as a planet orbits between its sun and Earth. Some of the language used was beyond the boy, but still, Walter found it... cool.

Mr. Hughes had spent half of last class talking about Kepler-186f. It was a planet located in the Cygnus constellation, about 490 light-years away. Very far as the crow flies but in space terms just a couple blocks away. It was one of the first planets to be discovered with an orbital radius similar to Earth's in the habitable zone of another star. According to experts, it was located in what was called the Goldilocks Zone, a reference to Goldilocks and the three bears. Too close to the sun: hot and unlivable. Too far away: cold and unlivable. It was just the right distance away, in this case, in the orbit of a small red dwarf. It was the first of many such discoveries in the last few years.

Walter could hear another dog barking, this time on the other side of the reserve. It sounded like one of his Uncle Dick's hounds. He hoped it wouldn't be at it all night. Studying the sky, he managed to find Cygnus. He had learned that much in class. Somewhere in that group of stars sat Kepler-186f. His teacher had said there was still a lot more to learn about the planet, but the fact that it might be Earth-like, and support life, was just amazing. Were there boys there, discontent or otherwise? Did they have the same dreams and problems as the ones here on Earth did?

Walter sighed. He hoped life there—if it did exist—was a little more interesting, and happier, than life down here. Lying there on the mound of dirt, he closed his eyes and wished he could send his spirit up into the heavens.

*　*　*

Eric hated the *thump thump thump* of the atmospherics. They were so loud and the vibrations rattled across the whole settlement, all four square kilometres of it. No matter where you were in the huge octagonal enclosure, you could always feel the repetitive shudder as the atmospherics converted the indigenous atmosphere into oxygen. Most citizens had grown used to it and barely noticed the rumbling anymore, but for some reason Eric could feel every single tremor every single time. Lying in bed, he could count the seconds between each successive boom—usually four and a half—and then the next one would sound.

His bunk, inserted ergonomically into the wall at the back of his father's locale (the new Keplerspeak for "apartment"). While functional in the optimal usage of apartment space, it barely gave him room to turn over in frustration. Tonight, like most nights, sleep was eluding him, chased away by the constant heartbeat of Plymroc. The name, with its connections to Old Earth, was a contraction of Plymouth Rock, a symbolic name for this new and daring settlement on a foreign planet.

Feeling exasperated by his sensitivity, Eric rose and put on his jumpsuit. It looked like it would be another night of wandering the hallways and labs of Plymroc until he tired himself out and forced his body to sleep. He thought this even though he knew exactly where he was going. He went there every night he couldn't sleep. One of the technicians had even given him the security code, remarking that Eric almost spent more time there than he did.

As expected, twenty Kepler minutes later, Eric showed up at the Astronosphere. He considered this place the doorway to the galaxy. Inside its walls, the young man could access all aspects of the galaxy in a few minutes, though that was a misnomer. Time was a tricky concept in the world of astronomy. Light-years were not a measurement of time but of distance. And in the four or five minutes it would take him to load the computers and access any one of the numerous technological arrays that scanned the heavens, the information he would be looking at would be hours, weeks, years, more than likely millenniums old. But the important thing was he could look at them now, regardless of when the visible light or gamma rays or x-rays had begun their journey across the universe.

Eric's father, like many people in the settlement, had several responsibilities. He worked in hydroponics as well as metallurgical structuring. The founders of Plymroc felt that focusing on one field of expertise for the rest of your life, so far away from most Earth-like diversions, could create psychological problems. So most Keplerites juggled two professions to keep the mind active. This way, each individual could flex different parts of their cognizance.

His father had never noticed Eric's midnight absences. He was always too busy or too tired. Although it was twenty-two years old, the settlement of Plymroc was far from complete. It was a never-ending construction site, with priority given to such necessities as atmospherics upgrades and water purification. Right now, the list on the original Schedule of Priorities drawn up on landing was only two-thirds finished. It was estimated another twelve to fourteen years were needed before the framework of the settlement would be finalized. It would be that long before his father and many of the other colonists would be released from their twelve-hour workdays. Eric's mother had died not long after he was born, what with the med centre being less of a priority than the atmospherics and biofood domes.

As he had expected, the Astronosphere was empty. In an attempt to mimic Earth as much as possible, Plymroc founders kept the normal terrestrial manifestations of time on Kepler-186f. The rotation of the planet was only fifty-six minutes longer, so it didn't take much of an effort to adapt it. Plymroc was on night shift now, so he had the lab to himself, as usual.

The Astronosphere was one of the few locations in the settlement specially shielded against the pervasive pulsations of the atmospherics. Because of the delicate nature of the equipment it contained, the room had been precisely designed to act as a buffer against man- and Kepler-made vibrations—the planet had a unique hum because of pulsations emanating from its highly crystalline core. For that reason, Eric had found great peace in the Cosmicon, short for Cosmic Consciousness. The Cosmicon was a small room within the Astronosphere with digital readouts and input monitors scattered in all six directions. If you manipulated things correctly—which Eric was very adept at—you could almost make it look like you were deep in space, alone and floating, surrounded by everything the Big Bang had spit out. Making himself comfortable in the Cosmicon, Eric booted the familiar program and adjusted the levels.

For about seven months now, since he had learned and decoded the programming behind the Cosmicon, he'd been able to shut out the outside world and manoeuvre himself through the far reaches of space. Floating below him in the inkiness was the Crab Nebula; dangling overhead was the distorted Orion's Belt. To his right, the twin suns of Sirius. To his left, a magnification of the massive black hole at the centre of the galaxy. And directly ahead, a strange, far-off place called Earth.

Of course, Eric had never been there. He'd been born several years after Plymroc was founded, but he'd heard the stories of the Origin. The elders of the community even jokingly referred to their exodus as "the Origin Express." Few now got the joke. Eric had visited the archival web, as well as taken the yearly courses in school. Every resident had studied Earth's history, composition, location and people in school, and he had studied far more by himself, in here, alone. Although the planet was far and remote, he held it close and personal. He sure wished he could see an elephant in the flesh, but that was most definitely unlikely to happen.

It was the SATD that got the first settlers here—Space Altering Thrust Drive. It altered the fabric of space, allowing transit in a remarkably short time—though, again, time is relative. It took 490 years for light from Earth's yellow sun to reach Kepler, and it would have taken double, triple, quadruple that amount of time for a spaceship to traverse that distance by conventional means. The SATD took only twenty years, the problem being it was a one-way trip. The drive burns itself out. The citizens of Plymroc could try to build another one to return with, but why? They would travel for twenty years to settle this planet, only to spend five years and much of their limited resources building a new SATD, then travel for another twenty years to return to Earth. Not much point in all that.

Eric knew every nuance and shade of that far-off blue planet. Kepler-186f had more of a dull greenish-grey tinge to it, unlike Earth's fabulous bright cerulean. It was unlikely he would ever set foot on Earth, but there was no harm in visiting it with his eyes or mind.

The image in front of him had taken 490 years to reach Kepler-186f. Again, in galactic terms, that wasn't very long. The Earth he was looking at was very different from the Earth he knew was there now. It was like looking into a time machine. When the sun's light had bounced off the planet's surface and begun its journey across the cosmos to this hidden part of the galaxy, the human race had not even flown in planes yet. It was just a hundred or so years after somebody named Columbus had sailed across what had been thought of as an impenetrable ocean, navigating by the stars, and landed on a continent populated by people who no doubt had their own ideas about the stars and planets far above them.

Once Columbus had landed, colonies had spread, and eventually people from those same colonies had crossed what they thought was an even more difficult and impenetrable terrain—the vastness of space.

Maybe right now, looking up at him from somewhere down on that faraway planet, was another young man just like him, looking up at the heavens, stargazing.

Wouldn't that be something, Eric thought.

SUPERDISAPPOINTED

Kyle Muncy woke that morning as he did every morning, with a weary resignation and a general reluctance to open his eyes and face the day. His logic being that once his eyes became naked and were forced to focus on the world around him, his day would have to begin, and no doubt end just as dismally. "Colour you blue," his lawyer would frequently joke. Somewhat embarrassed, Kyle had to look up the word, but in the end he had to agree. Disillusionment was such an unfortunate state of mind for the world's first Aboriginal superhero.

As a child, he had devoured comic books and cartoons about characters that through any varied number of experiences had ended up like him. In his teenage years, the television shows had promised a life of adventure and heroism. The adult years had provided movies glorifying the acts of those gifted and blessed with powers not possessed by the majority of the population. But, he told himself these days, he was not the first Native person—super or otherwise—to be lied to by the dominant culture.

Once again, Kyle focused on his sealed eyelids. Under normal circumstances—though few things in his life could be called normal—his lids had the kinetic power to lift small horses, should such a need ever arise. At present, it was his will that was lacking. Thus, with great mental effort and the knowledge that putting off the inevitable was useless, Kyle made the choice to start his day. Hesitantly, he contracted the enhanced muscles that operated his lids, and light from all parts of the spectrum flooded his eyes. His immediate empire was once again revealed to him. This realm consisted of a weathered fifty-four-year-old one-bedroom house located on the edge of the Otter Lake First Nation, a community that prior to his conversion to mythic status had been virtually unknown to the country at large. Below him was a small basement crammed with generations of family clutter. Above him, a patched roof barely kept the elements at bay. He greeted this familiar reality with a weary sigh. It was another day to do battle with. Just another stretch of time for dealing with all the crap that now accompanied his superlife.

Every muscle in his body was ridiculously powered, but Kyle moved like a tired old man, though in reality he was thirty, as regular humans measured time. It wasn't gravity that ate away at his nimbleness, because he had long ago conquered such a pedestrian natural element. Instead, it was a psychological lassitude that seemed to weigh down his body, the kind he'd seen in his grandfather during his later years. The man had nine kids, a low-paying job most of his life and a series of repeated minor and major crises that always seemed to spring out of nowhere. When he died, his grandson thought he could see a smile on the old man's now-peaceful face as the lid of the casket was lowered.

Kyle sighed again and finally rose from his single bed. The bed had been a present from his parents almost twelve years ago. It was practically the newest thing in his modest house. As if making some sort of ironic statement regarding the hoarding of precious Aboriginal artifacts by museums around the world, his home was littered with numerous refugees from the twentieth century. Along the back wall sat a sizable collection of eight-track tapes. Underneath a small coffee table by the window sat both a fax machine and a rotary phone. And so on. It seemed his house was where that century had gone to die.

Like most people in the world, the man got dressed and performed his morning ablutions. He made and ate his breakfast. Brushed his teeth. Did all the usual things everybody else in the world does who doesn't have superstrength and the ability to fly. He was practically invulnerable, but for the thousandth time he wished he could get a haircut. An unexpected side effect of his condition. Same with shaving. He had to manually pull the hairs out of his chin. Luckily, being Aboriginal limited the amount of growth, but still, it was a painful and annoying affair.

It would be a long day, for there were things to do and errands to run for this man of amazing abilities. First on his agenda: hitchhiking into town. Standing there along Highway 48, his thumb out, he found himself looking up. Far overhead, Kyle could see the condensation trails of a high-flying jet. Yes, he knew it would be so much easier and quicker to fly into town, like he used to do when it first began. Snap your fingers and he'd be walking down the main street before the dust had settled on his dirt driveway. But that, like so many things, was then. And then was not now. Still, he had his superthumb.

Twenty-two minutes later.

"Hey, you that guy with all those superpowers?" Kyle climbed in.

The large man driving the truck looked like any man who spent most of his time sitting in pickups eating fast food. The floor of the vehicle looked like a dozen university students had partied in a mall food court and left the remnants behind for a future archaeologist to decipher. Amid all the wrappers and cardboard, Kyle couldn't see his weathered sneakers. The man, whose name was Karl if his vanity licence plate was correct, took another look at his passenger.

"Huh? That you?"

Kyle had been in this position many times before and dreaded the upcoming questions. "Yeah, that's me."

The driver looked genuinely excited. "Why you hitchhiking, then? I thought you could fly."

"Yeah, I can."

Karl, if that was his name, looked like he was wrestling with calculating pi. "Like I said, then why…?"

Kyle was quick with his answer. "It's a long story. But the municipal airport is so close…" At that moment, up ahead on the north side, a small plane could be seen climbing over the distant trees. "…and I've had three—they say it was four, but they're wrong… I'm pretty sure it was only three—near collisions."

The driver made a hard right turn and all the refuse on the floor seemed to shift and slide as a whole. "No shit?"

A squirrel did a shoulder roll into the ditch as the truck powered by.

"No shit. Since then I've been asked not to fly within the county lines, under penalty of law. And some people claim some of the local cows get nervous when they see me flying by. Farmers say they stop giving milk."

"And that's why you hitchhike?"

Kyle took a deep breath before answering. "Yeah."

It took an unusually long moment for Karl to gather his thoughts. "That sucks."

"Yeah. It does."

In addition, there was a rare and protected bird of some sort nesting in the nearby trees, and there was concern Kyle's flying might be a hazard to it. Kyle thought it best not to say anything more about the issue and, despite Karl's repeated attempts to converse with the celebrity in his truck, spent the remainder of the trip into town nursing his silence.

On both sides of the vehicle, almost two dozen farms of every description whizzed by. Some corn- and hay-based, others more concerned with animal husbandry. Kyle could see, hear and smell pigs, cows, chickens, alpacas and something else that was foreign to his supersensitive nose. It all looked so peaceful.

Following his arrival in the mid-sized community of Bayfield, there were three important errands he needed to accomplish that day, the reason for his sojourn from the safety and anonymity of his small house into the harsh light of this municipality's curiosity. First and foremost, a long-awaited conversation with Raymond Laurier, owner of the Bright Morning Café. He'd been dreading this for a while, but it was a talk that was a long time coming.

As usual, Raymond was behind the dessert case putting out what appeared to be raspberry cheesecake and some sort of apple crumble. It was still early and the place was empty. Looking lean and fit, the man seemed just as tasty to the superhero as the sweets he was peddling. As Kyle opened the door, Raymond looked up with the smile he used for customers. It disappeared upon recognition of Kyle, and then a different kind of smile was substituted.

Two minutes later.

"Kyle…"

Kyle returned a similar smile and joined his boyfriend… former boyfriend… he wasn't sure which was more accurate right now. That's why he was here.

"I wish you'd phoned and let me know you were coming into town."

Raymond didn't seem as overjoyed to see him as Kyle had hoped. In fact, he seemed kind of nervous. Perhaps that's why they were sitting at the small table in the back, near the bathrooms. Above them on a sturdy-looking ledge hung a number of sizable tennis trophies, all bearing Raymond's name.

The super-Aboriginal drank his coffee, enjoying a heat that would scald most humans. "I was gonna, but I'm fairly sure my phone is tapped. You know how things are…"

Raymond lifted his coffee cup and then put it back down. Too hot for his mortal mouth. "Aren't you being a little paranoid? I thought most of the stuff with the government had died down and everybody was letting you live your life… normally."

"As normally as possible" was what Raymond was probably thinking. Kyle didn't comment. He added four more tablespoons of sugar to his coffee. With his accelerated metabolism, he needed a lot more calories than the average person.

"First thing I do practically every morning, once I crawl out of bed, is throw a couple rocks up at the sky and bring down as many of those stupid drones that are always circling my place as possible. With my hearing the way it is, I can barely sleep. No wonder they're called drones."

For a moment, Raymond touched Kyle's hand in sympathy, then just as quickly he returned his hand to his side of the table.

"I don't know if they're the government, or the press, or just people curious to get a peek at me."

Automatically Raymond looked out the front picture window, half expecting to see something hovering there. Not yet.

"Unfortunately, there's nothing I can do about that satellite hovering a couple hundred kilometres over my place," Kyle said as he took another sip of coffee. "I mean, yeah, I could, but that would probably get me in a lot more trouble."

Now Raymond managed a small chuckle. "Now that sounds like paranoia for sure."

Kyle shook his head. "Nope. I can see it. One of the solar panels has a hole in it. Probably from some meteor or space shit. But it's there." He looked up, as if he wanted to see the satellite again through the mauve-coloured ceiling. Instead, he broached the reason he'd come to the café. "Ray, I haven't seen you in a while."

Luckily, the café was still empty and nobody else could see the mortal man shift uncomfortably in his seat. "Things have been busy."

Kyle looked around at the empty chairs. "Uh-huh. I can tell."

Staring down at the pale-blue tablecloth, Raymond searched for the right words to say to the man whose bed and heart he had once shared. "Kyle, I'm too old for all this. My days of sneaking around are long gone. Even with somebody like you. Yes, I know it's been a while since we got together, but you're just as much to blame as I am. I mean… I've been waiting for you to acknowledge me in your life. I was part of it before, and I wanted to be part of it again."

Of all the inconveniences of being super, being forced apart from Raymond had been the hardest to bear, and Kyle could bear a lot—after all, he was bear clan. There was a time when the man across from him had brought him strength; now the superstrength he had was keeping them apart. Theirs was a history going back six years. A lot had happened in those six years. But the last eighteen months had proven too much for their relationship to survive.

"Ray, you know…"

"What do I know, Kyle, what? That you had your chance? God knows you've had a million chances to share me with the world. You couldn't fart without it making the media. And now, to tell you the truth, I don't know if I want you to acknowledge me. It's too late." There. It was out in the open.

Kyle responded by trying to be as positive as he could. "Look, Ray, I can only come out of so many closets at once. I came out of the superhero closet when all this stuff happened to me and told the world who and what I was, and look what happened. It became a circus. If I tell people I'm gay, too… Well, things will go crazy again. For me and for you. For different reasons. That's why—"

Raymond responded with a shot of honesty that stopped Kyle cold. "I understand. I truly do. That's why… I… I think we should go our separate ways. You need time. We both do."

Somehow, Kyle wasn't as surprised as he would have thought he'd be. Some part of him must have known this was coming. Maybe he was developing precognition as a new power.

Raymond continued. "I don't like the spotlight, you know that. I've got this business to look after and you… Well, you've got a shitload of your own things to work out, personally and privately. I can only imagine what you're going through… None of this is your fault. I just think it's more than me and you can deal with, Kyle. I'm sorry."

Kyle was silent for a moment. Then he reached across and gently squeezed Raymond's hand. "Is that the only reason?"

Raymond squeezed Kyle's hand back. "Well, if what the doctor says is true and your muscles will keep getting stronger and stronger, there's no telling what could happen. Ray, you're still a work-in-progress…, in every sense of the word."

Abruptly, Kyle stood up, understanding the game had changed. No use whining about it. "You're right. You're absolutely right. Well, I gotta go. Have a good life, Ray. I really do mean that."

Before Raymond could respond, the man he had once loved was out the door and gone like some old-time hero disappearing into the sunset. On the table in front of him was what was left of the ceramic coffee cup that Kyle had cradled, then crushed into a fine powder.

"Poor Kyle," muttered Raymond as he turned to get a dustpan and brush.

That was that, and now it was over. Just another pothole in the road of Kyle's life. Things have to get better, he thought.

Seventeen minutes later.

"It's not looking good, Kyle."

Then again, it was never good when Kyle visited his lawyer. Just once, he'd like to walk into the woman's second-floor office and be told something positive. The so-called "law of averages" dictated that occasionally, even rarely, there had to be some good news emanating from all his legal tribulations. But unfortunately, his lawyer didn't practise that brand of law.

"Which case are we talking about this time?"

In reality, there were a number of legal issues stemming from Kyle's status as an Aboriginal superhero. Also in reality, there was no possible way he could afford to have a full-time lawyer see to all his legal needs. Luckily, Amelia Staebler found the Native man's situation interesting and had offered her services pro bono. Well, maybe pro bono wasn't quite the correct term. She was writing a book about the legal implications of superherodom, with Kyle as her lab rat... or muskrat, in accordance with his Aboriginal heritage. She found things like that funny.

Deep inside the hard drive of her computer, she located Kyle's file. "Where to begin... Well, let's start with that high school and those Junior A teams. They don't want to settle. They want to go to court. Surprise, surprise, huh?"

Kyle let out a supersigh. "Chrissake, I used to like baseball and hockey."

"Yeah, but they don't like you."

When Kyle had first manifested superpowers, he'd wanted to use them for good, like all the traditional superheroes he'd grown up reading about. Save damsels in distress, stop planes from crashing, shore up cracked dams, help kittens down from trees—all the normal stuff like that. That was his goal, anyway. But they're called goals because they may be aimed for but not necessarily achieved. Something he was now bitterly aware of.

So you couldn't be a decent and respected superhero without a decent and respected superhero name. Thus, he'd adopted the name Thunderbird, in honour of his heritage. Turned out this was a bad choice. Nearly a dozen sports teams were already using the name and felt Kyle's international fame as the so-called Thunderbird was an infringement on their trademark. These were the first of many such lawsuits.

"I'm still working out the depositions, but it's not looking good, I'm sorry to say. They seem quite rabid."

At times, he tried to figure out if there were some undertones of racism in these lawsuits. After all, he didn't remember Superman or Spider-Man or the Hulk going through all this. Or possibly the world just wasn't ready for all the social, legal and moral implications of an honest-to-goodness, real-life superhero. Otherwise he wouldn't so ardently need the services of Bayfield's best legal mind. Because, as luck would have it, this hero happened to be a gay First Nations man. But with his community college education, he eventually decided to leave those questions to those who get paid to ponder these things.

"So what else?" he asked.

Ms. Staebler went through a litany of complaints, suits and cases. There was the bank just down the street that wanted him to compensate them for the wall and the vault he had destroyed while foiling a bank robbery. It seemed their insurance didn't cover acts of superstrength. And there were the Gilmans, who held him responsible for the heart attack of their elderly father, who was the first person to see him fly. Even his own community was distancing itself from him. After so many decades of trying to force their way into Canadian society by saying they as First Nations people were no different from and deserved the same rights as all Canadians, somebody like Kyle Muncy came along and threw a wrench into that argument. Add to that all the crazies and religious fanatics that either wanted to destroy him as a threat to humanity or worship him as some sort of messiah or god, and things were becoming difficult, and potentially dangerous, for the locals. Of course, there was also the matter of that aggressive children's advocacy group that held him responsible for all the injuries suffered by numerous children trying to imitate him flying, going through walls, and stopping cars and bullets. The list was staggering.

"I don't know why I'm to blame for kids being so stupid. Don't they know I have no money?"

The smartly dressed woman leaned back in her chair. "I don't think it's necessarily about the money. They all know your financial situation. Any luck finding work?"

Kyle shrugged. "Not really. Seems I'm tainted. Who'd wanna hire me? I still get an offer or two a week from these far-off countries I can't pronounce, all wanting my help taking over the world. But I really don't want to leave home."

"That's... that's probably a good thing." She coughed into her hand. "Look, Kyle, I would normally tell somebody in your position to hang tough, but since you are the strongest man in the world there's not much point in saying that." She let out a short chuckle at her own joke. "I'm doing what I can, but when you're special like you obviously are, people sometimes dislike that. In fact, as I'm sure you've realized, quite a few downright resent it."

No wonder she wanted to paint him the colour blue.

"But I didn't ask for this. I never wanted this. I just want to disappear."

"You'd be surprised how many people say that in my office." Amelia managed a weak smile that did nothing to lift her client's spirits.

They tied up a few more legal odds and ends, and then Kyle left the lawyer's office for his next appointment. As he descended the flight of stairs to the ground floor, he could hear her typing away on her computer, feverishly writing up notes on their meeting, no doubt to be featured in her upcoming book.

Twenty-eight minutes later.

"Right on time, as usual. How are you feeling today, Kyle?"

Last on the list: Dr. Gary Sparco, general practitioner and doctor to all the superheroes in the county. This, of course, meant just Kyle. The portly and mostly bald man seemed genuinely happy to see the man literally hovering in his examination room.

"Same as always," he said, punctuating his declaration with a shrug.

His words were almost lost in the hissing sound of the doctor taking his blood pressure, which was usually a futile endeavour. The results frequently didn't make much sense or contradicted the previous visit's recorded reading, but it was habit for the good doctor. Once, Kyle had somehow broken the doctor's automated blood pressure machine, so now Dr. Sparco took it manually. The portable ones were easier to replace.

Today, it seemed Kyle's blood pressure was 80 over 120, which was the opposite of most people and generally considered impossible.

"Kyle, one day you're going to send me to an early grave. You realize you don't make sense—at least your body doesn't. I'm telling you, you need a specialist."

On the far side of town, Kyle could hear a car screeching to a stop and a dog barking at the car in annoyance.

"You're tellin' me there's a specialist for my condition? That's news to me. Yeah, everybody wants to prod and poke me, run tests, and try and keep me in a lab to study. Goddammit! My lawyer got rich off fighting that one. Naw, you've been my doctor since I can remember. There's more to being a doctor than just how much medicine you know. There's also trust. And I trust you."

Sitting down in front of his patient, the doctor did a quick visual survey of Kyle. Eyes looked good. Skin tone customary. Hair not falling out. Regular respiration. To Sparco, Kyle looked maddeningly normal and healthy.

"Wish I had your faith in me, Kyle, but as usual, I'll do my best. Any new symptoms or abilities to report?"

"Well, I think I'm beginning to attract animals. I'm not sure, but for the last week or so, there have been a whole lot of earthworms crawling up out of the ground around my house. Hundreds. Thousands. And as a result, lots and lots of robins have been swooping down on my lawn to eat them. Now, I've lived in that house forever, and I'm pretty sure that's not normal." He paused for a second. "Kinda annoying, actually."

Dr. Sparco wrote something down on Kyle's chart, shaking his head ever so slightly.

"Spontaneous abilities still manifesting themselves. I don't even know how to categorize this one. Possibly pheromones of some sort, but I'll add it to the list and do some research later. Okay, let me check the back of your throat."

Kyle opened his mouth wide and discovered he could disconnect his jaw at will now.

"This is also new," muttered the good doctor as he peered down the man's throat. "That's enough, Kyle. You can… close your mouth now."

Kyle did as he was told, and his jaw slipped back into place. "Well?"

The doctor put his clipboard down and swivelled in his chair to face the patient. "Well, what? You know that even after all this time, this is as new and bizarre to me as it is to you. I don't know what to tell you, Kyle. We've run what tests we can, which as you know is difficult in itself. We can't draw blood because of that damn puncture-proof skin. So we're reduced to doing what we can with saliva, urine and stool samples. Your urine eats through our plastic and glass containers, so that makes things extra tricky."

The lights in the room momentarily flickered. Kyle hoped it wasn't him.

"Can you at least tell me whether I'm getting better or worse?"

On the wall behind Dr. Sparco was a line of cartoonish body charts illustrating various organ and circulatory systems. Kyle had glanced at them on his first visit to the doctor's office and had long since memorized them. Another side effect of his condition.

"I don't know. You keep manifesting new abilities all the time. So far, none of them are overly injurious to other people or yourself, but that may be only for now. And then you lose other ones. You no longer glow in the dark, as far as I can tell, so that's something. Other… I don't know what you would call them… powers… don't change. It's hard to tell." The man looked frustrated. "This is new territory. I wish I could tell you more."

The room went silent, as silent as any room could be with Kyle's superhearing. Somebody not far away, just a block or two, was shouting out answers to a *Family Feud* episode.

"Kyle…?"

Kyle looked up.

"I'm sorry. You had such high hopes. You wanted to make a difference."

Kyle nodded, touched by the older man's empathy. "I talked to this elder on my reserve a few days ago. You know, looking for help trying to figure things out. Didn't know what he could offer me, him not being a particularly scientific kind of guy. But I'm getting pretty desperate…"

"What did he say?"

Outside the window, clouds had overtaken the sun and the world had become a little gloomier. On the doctor's desk was a four-inch-long quartz crystal. Kyle picked it up, savouring the cold, glassy feeling in his hand.

"He told me that he was taught that we were the land and the land was us. In a perfect world, we were to reflect each other. And if something is wrong with the Earth, then it makes sense that something will be wrong with us. It kind of makes sense, don't you think?"

Living so close to a First Nations community, Sparco had always tried to keep an open mind about traditional Native beliefs. A good many modern medicines came from compounds originally developed by these so-called "primitive" people. So he nodded, wondering where the conversation was going.

Gently squeezing the crystal, Kyle continued talking, remembering the conversation he'd had the preceding Sunday. "He thought maybe I was the Earth fighting back. I'm the first casualty of a war to come."

"What does that mean?"

"I don't know. I stopped trying to figure any of this out a long time ago." Turning the cloudy semi-precious stone slowly in his hand, Kyle counted the six sides of smooth, angular coldness. "Why am I the way I am, Doctor?"

Dr. Sparco wasn't sure he was comfortable with where the conversation was going. "Kyle, you know we aren't sure…"

"But there are theories, aren't there?"

"Of course there are. There are always theories, but——"

"But some make more sense than others, don't they? Okay, Doctor, after all these tests and examinations, why do you think I am the way I am? You've read all the reports on the tests the government did, the tests you've done, all the resources of our fine society… Why am I the way I am? Why am I?"

The doctor bit his lower lip. He had nothing to hide. This wasn't a massive government conspiracy. Still, like every doctor worth his salt, Sparco was not fond of delivering bad news. He'd become a doctor specifically with the hopes of delivering as much good news as possible. Today was not going to be such a day. "It's complicated." He wasn't sure where to go from there.

Kyle held up the quartz and looked through it at the squat, malformed figure of the doctor on the other side. "The world is complicated. Why should this be any different? I just want to hear you say it."

Reluctantly, Sparco leaned across his desk and grabbed the Muncy file. His chair creaked loudly in protest. He remembered when Kyle was a little boy and had broken his wrist falling from a tree. Another time, Kyle's head had required four stitches due to playing baseball. A third time, his thumb had gotten infected by an errant piece of glass. Knowing Kyle's parents had passed on not long ago and that he was alienated from most of his community, Sparco felt for the simple man with godlike powers. And now his patient was holding firmly in his hand the piece of quartz Sparco's grandson had given him. Despite everything, it seemed the Aboriginal man still possessed some of his childlike fascination with the world. Sparco hated to ruin that.

"Well, ahem, as far as we know, it is possible that your environment was largely responsible for your... metamorphosis."

Kyle knocked the quartz three times on the table, creating an echoing effect. "That's what I don't get. Most of what all these doctors and scientists theorize I don't really understand. I live in a small house on a reserve with a thousand other people. Why me? Why not them? Why not anybody else?" His voice rose and his fist clamped down on the crystal.

Although he wasn't afraid of the young man, Sparco was... he would say... concerned about his emotional outburst. "As I said, it's complicated. It's been theorized that the water you drink—"

"The substandard water most of my community is forced to drink? That water?!"

This was a contentious issue. Like many other First Nations communities across the country, Muncy's reserve was under a contaminated water alert. Had been for the past seven years, at least. That's when the toxins had first been discovered in the groundwater. Who knows how long they'd been there? Local Native people were pissed off about this, and the doctor was well aware of the ill effects of unclean water. But as his patient had been asking ever since his metamorphosis had begun, why him?

"Yes, that water. With all the chemicals and impurities that have been digested by your body..."

Kyle remembered the farms he'd passed driving into the city with Karl. "The stuff from all that agriculture, right?"

The doctor nodded. "The fertilizers, antibiotics, growth hormones and steroids they give to the animals eventually make it into the water table. And then into you."

Kyle was silent for a moment. "What else?"

Flipping over a sheet of paper, Dr. Sparco's eyes scanned the test results. "Well, and this is just conjecture, you realize, there's all the radon gas that was found saturating your house. As you know, that stuff is a natural by-product of the decay of radium and is radioactive."

"Yeah, I've heard all this before, but nobody will tell me how my house could have become saturated with this radon gas. This doesn't sound… normal."

"It is normal, Kyle. It's… it's naturally occurring. I've told you this. Seeps up through the ground. I know it sounds weird, but it's true. Because of that, a lot of places have radon gas detectors."

Kyle took a deep breath. "But not on my reserve?"

"So it seems. And somehow, someway, the gas and the steroids and the fertilizers interacted with your biology, bonding and transforming your body on a cellular level, creating all sorts of unique… side effects. We're not quite sure how… exactly."

It's a good thing Kyle wasn't a gambling man, thought Sparco, or he'd be broke and in jail by now. The Gods of Chance didn't seem to be too fond of his patient. Actually, on second thought, broke and in jail might be a little better than Kyle's current situation.

"Anything else?"

When Kyle had first come into his office eighteen months ago, when he first began manifesting these unique abilities, the doctor had been amazed, possibly even a little envious. Over the decades, he'd seen a lot of damaged bodies and persistent illnesses, and now here in front of him was a man it seemed God and the universe had made indestructible, even superior. The good doctor was now quite sure he'd been overly generous in his assessment of Kyle Muncy and his condition. If you have all the money in the world but no place to spend it, is there a point?

"Yes, one other thing. It seems all that black mould in your house also contributed to your… condition."

By now, Kyle was getting weary. He wanted to know the details, but each statement of fact made him feel like a tree with a persistent lumberjack, each scientific declaration a swing from a sharp and heavy axe.

"The black mould?"

Sparco put the chart down on his desk and removed his glasses. He slid his chair a little closer to his patient. "Seems like the spores of the black mould acted as some sort of organic catalyst within your system. Somehow they helped metabolize all the other elements into... into... into what you are."

In the park nearby, Kyle could hear children laughing. He could smell chili, today's special, at the restaurant across the road. In the building next door, somebody was playing their stereo, and Dr. Sparco's unusual patient could feel the *thump thump* of the bass. Sounded like something by The Doors.

"I suppose that makes sense."

Suddenly his own office seemed very small to the doctor. "Actually, it doesn't. That's why we need to do more tests and—"

"Thanks, Doctor, I'll think about it." It had been a long day for the reluctant superhero. And it would be a long hitchhike back in the growing darkness. Kyle made his departure quick.

"I know this all sounds..."

There was no ending to the sentence, as the patient had exited the office, leaving behind a conflicted man of medicine. Stepping out of the building onto the street out front was the most amazing person humanity and nature had managed to create together. Everybody should have been doing cartwheels. Instead, there were no cartwheels in Kyle's life. Sparco closed the file on his most interesting patient and replaced it in his desk drawer. Nothing frustrates a doctor more than a sense of medical impotency. Actually, Sparco could cure most types of impotency... but not this kind.

Late that night, Kyle Muncy crawled into bed. The day was over. The only thing he had looked forward to all day was closing his eyes again, finding blissful nothingness until they opened once more. There was always the hope that tomorrow might be better. Otherwise, this was just another day in the life of a superhero.

Kyle Muncy, the first Aboriginal superhero, closed his eyes and slept, peaceful for the first time that day.

Meanwhile, across the Earth, terrible people were doing terrible things, to themselves and to the planet. These terrible events were happening non-stop, with nobody to help prevent them. And in another part of the damaged world, someone else struggling to survive was discovering they had new, unexpected yet formidable powers, created from an unholy alliance of man-made environmental corruption and toxic natural elements.

And Kyle slept on.

TAKE US TO YOUR CHIEF

The men sitting on the couches in the middle of Old Man's Point didn't need the screeching of the cicadas to tell them how hot it was. The sweat on their foreheads and on the beer bottles gave them ample evidence. The sweat was cyclical: the more sweat on their foreheads, the more need for cold beer, which in turn became sweat in the humidity of the summer woods.

Old Man's Point was located near the eastern shore of Otter Lake, named for an old man who used to stand on the bank and point at all the boats going by. A deserted stretch of shoreline running parallel to a rarely used dirt road, it housed a group of cedar trees that grew skyward in a sort of amphitheatre configuration. Over the years, several worn and tattered couches had found their way to the cedars, which circled an ancient firepit. Weathered by many years of rain, snow, sun and sweaty Aboriginal behinds, the sofas looked as beaten down, as lived in and as much a part of the landscape as the men. The constant breeze from the lake kept the more persistent mosquitos and other bugs of July away, and all in all, it was a comfortable and picturesque place to pass the summer months.

Today, like most lazy days, there sat three Ojibway men. Tarzan, Cheemo and Teddy had been there since ten that morning, enjoying a cooler stocked with beer that was chilling in the shallow waters near the shore. They had no place to go and nothing much to do, a happy coincidence for all. Most of their relations agreed the trio were men of few words and fewer ambitions. And the three saw little need to argue. They did what they did, and they were very good at it.

Although they spent long hours in each other's company—they had been best buddies since their early school days—they said remarkably little. Several seasons back, a cousin had joined them for the day and had come away utterly bewildered.

"They didn't say anything. Not one word!" the cousin had exclaimed. "I tried to talk with them about something, anything, but I got nothing back. They would just sit there, look around occasionally, smile and drink beer. That's all." He never went back.

The men had spent so much time together over the years, they practically knew each other's thoughts; thus, nothing needed to be said. Besides, nothing much happened to them that needed to be discussed anyway.

Until the spaceship landed.

It was a Tuesday. Tarzan, so called because as a kid he loved running around the village and climbing trees in his underwear, was pulling three more beers out of the cooler when he heard it. Years sitting at Old Man's Point with his cousins had made him far more aural than oral. The buzzing of insects, the calls of birds, the lapping of water on the shore, the distant drone of motorboats constituted pretty much the only auditory landscape in the area. So when the insects and birds suddenly went quiet and the relative silence was filled by a growing humming sound—no, humming wasn't quite the right word, but it would have to do—Tarzan's curiosity was piqued. He looked to his right and then left. Not seeing anything out of the ordinary, he finally looked up, over the lake, and almost dropped his beer. Almost.

Cheemo, whose name tragically translates from Ojibway into English roughly as "Big Shit," heard the unfamiliar sound next. At first, Cheemo thought the noise was coming from a passing boat, but then it occurred to him boats don't usually pass overhead.

Puzzled, he looked over to his brother, Teddy, who since childhood had given off the vague aroma of puppy breath. As a result, children loved him. But Teddy's eyes were closed, as the wind had increased and he was enjoying the caresses of the midsummer breeze, for alas, those were the only caresses in his life. It took his baseball cap flying across the firepit and into the goldenrods near the edge of the clearing to make him open his eyes. What was fast approaching filled his eyes, but the rest of him refused to comprehend the large flashing, multicoloured object making a clear path to their couches. He closed his eyes for a second, thinking maybe it would disappear. No such luck, for he could see the flashing lights through his eyelids. Additionally, it was still there when he reopened them. Teddy shrugged and took a sip of beer.

By now the hum was constant and unmistakable. Cheemo could tell it was close, and judging from Tarzan's pose, head pointed ninety degrees straight up, it was directly overhead. Finally, putting two and two together, Cheemo looked up through the branches of the cedars to see what had caught his brother's and cousin's attention.

Although its shape seemed somewhat amorphous because it was glowing, the object was definitely round, and quite sizable. Perhaps as wide as four or five eighteen-wheelers lined up side by side, thought Cheemo, trying to render an unfamiliar and unexpected occurrence familiar and concrete. The other two expressed their earnest opinion by dropping their jaws, though oddly enough, neither was surprised enough to drop the beer bottle clutched in his hands.

Whatever it was grew closer, eventually descending onto the sandy beach adjacent to the nearby road. It landed not with a thud but with a soft whoosh as the air was pushed aside. A small cloud of road dust briefly surrounded the thing. The men's faces and bodies were bathed in the broad spectrum of colours emitted by the craft, a dozen different hues reflecting the spectrum of visible light, and possibly a few as yet undiscovered by the human race. Birds, insects, frogs and other animals local to Old Man's Point suddenly remembered they had plans elsewhere and evacuated. In a remarkably short period of time, it was just the strange object, the cedar trees and the three men left in the immediate area. It should be pointed out that in the forty or so seconds since they had spotted the approach of the mysterious craft, the men had not moved a centimetre.

A few more seconds passed as the humming seemed to lessen and the flashing of the lights diminished. Tarzan, somehow realizing this wasn't exactly a normal occurrence, glanced at Teddy, who in turn glanced at Cheemo. Finally, Cheemo managed to force his eyes off the craft and looked to Tarzan for any suggestion of what to do. Unfortunately, expert recommendations for handling such a unique situation were a rare commodity that morning in Otter Lake, and even scarcer in that little nook of the reserve. The only comment on the situation was a loud, nervous gulp by Teddy. The other two quickly followed suit.

Suddenly, the humming shifted, and the whirring lights froze. A new sound emerged from somewhere beneath the pulsating luminosity—a higher-pitched buzzing reminiscent of a thousand mosquitos filtered through a blown guitar amp. Then a rectangular patch of obsidian light erupted along one side of the craft, near the bottom. It flared briefly, then dissipated, revealing what appeared to the three men to be an opaque stairway of sorts. And more distressing, something seemed to be… the only word Tarzan could come up with was… flowing… down the mysterious ramp.

By now it had occurred to the Old Man's Point trio that perhaps this would be a good time to relocate to a less historic location and ponder their next course of action. However, before they could move, they heard a new sound. It was a watery, thick voice, one that seemed to be trying to find the correct boundaries of vocal expression. The sound was fuzzy for a few seconds before it solidified into something understandable.

"Greetings, people of Earth."

It had spoken to them. Cheemo looked to Teddy, unsure whether the voice was referring to them, for he was fairly sure they were people from Earth, but he didn't want to jump to conclusions. White people were always changing the names of things: countries, people and a bunch of other things. He wouldn't put it past them to change the name of the planet. He had seen on the news some time ago that Pluto was no longer considered a planet. It had been downgraded to the celestial equivalent of a non-status planet.

For obvious reasons, Teddy's attention was not on his brother. He was too busy wondering why it felt as if all his hair was standing on end, like when he forgot to put fabric softener sheets in the dryer.

Tarzan realized his beer was empty, and this was definitely a time for extra beer.

For a brief period, the only sound other than the peculiar humming was the casual lapping of water on the shore. Then more words came from the very strange stranger.

"We are the Kaaw Wiyaa. We come in peace."

That's good, thought Tarzan. Peace is always good.

More cognizant of the history-making implications of the event developing around them, Cheemo tried hard to focus and memorize all that was happening. He knew that, should they survive this encounter, there could be good money and a future of free beer on the horizon. But at the moment, it was difficult to make out who or what was actually talking. Much like the craft, the defining boundaries around the individual seemed to be disobeying the rule that light travels in a straight line. Occasionally, he glimpsed what he thought were tentacles.

Calamari, thought Cheemo, I haven't had calamari in a long time.

There was a constant shimmering, and intermittently what appeared to be dark or smoky blobs emerged in the general vicinity of the strange being.

Must be a bitch taking a family photo, thought Teddy.

Tarzan couldn't help thinking what a cool effect this was. Must freak the girls out.

"You are citizens of this planet?"

All three took a reasonable guess and nodded. Remembering his mother's frequent comments about hospitality and politeness, Cheemo wondered if he should offer... it... a beer... then thought better of the idea. They only had three left. And he wasn't sure that thing had a mouth. Or a liver. Or a bladder.

"Excellent. We wish to open diplomatic negotiations with your planet. That is why we wish to see your leader."

Mentally, Cheemo was kicking himself. He should have watched more *Star Trek* as a kid. *Star Wars* doesn't really prepare you for a situation like this. This was definitely a *Star Trek* moment.

Meanwhile, Tarzan was wondering if they'd let him drive their... spaceship. There was this ex-girlfriend's house he'd like to hover over, maybe dump some interstellar garbage on.

"Will you take us to your leader, then?"

Grabbing the initiative, Cheemo nodded. This was not their problem. This is what people get elected for and why they enjoy those luxurious band office salaries. In those few short seconds, Cheemo had decided a life of fortune and fame just wasn't for him. He preferred the under-the-radar, low-stress approach. And he was fairly confident the other two would agree. Almost as if reading his mind, Teddy was nodding his head, agreeing with Cheemo via a lifelong cultural practice of not contradicting family when you have nothing better to say.

In reality, Teddy was wondering if that thing with calamari arms had farted. He was fairly sure he could smell a fart, but not one he had ever smelled before. And the nature of the breeze indicated it was coming from the direction of the newcomer. Unfortunately, Teddy's Grade 10 chemistry class twenty years ago had neglected to teach him about the prevalence of methane in the universe, and that many planets, including several in his own solar system, contained large quantities of methane. Some scientists have even theorized that alien life would breathe it the same way the ecosystem on Earth uses oxygen. Methane has the same approximate chemical makeup of certain gastrointestinal by-products in Earth animals. Through its unique physiology and the atmosphere it breathed, the Kaaw Wiyaa smelled constantly of a fart.

As for the "take me to your leader" part, Cheemo glanced at Tarzan who glanced at Teddy who glanced back at Cheemo. They all knew where to take him.

It was 3:36 on a hot, gorgeous Tuesday and, luckily, the chief of the Otter Lake First Nation was in his office, not whacking huge divots in the piece of Mother Earth his community had sold to a golf course two decades ago. It took some manoeuvring to get the sizable and abundantly limbed Kaaw Wiyaa through the band office door. It had recently been remodelled to be wheelchair accessible, but not quite alien accessible. And as they'd passed him in the hall, the janitor had looked worriedly at the trail of slime it was leaving on his newly cleaned carpets. For this he got a degree in Indigenous Studies?

Chief Angus Benojee, a man expanding at the belly but thinning on top, sat in his leather chair staring at the creature his nephews had brought into his office. His skinny little moustache quivered in a combination of confusion and irritation. There was barely enough room in the small office for the three men and… it. Tarzan, the smallest of the three, had to climb up on a table and sit cross-legged—Indian-style, some would say—so that the others could comfortably fit. To make things worse, the chief was certain somebody had farted.

"I am honoured to meet the leader of this great planet."

The chief's brow furrowed. This was his third term in office and this took the cake for most unusual meeting of the year, beating out by far his lunch with the acting regional director for Governmental Interdepartmental Subsidies and Regional Financial Accessibility (ARD-GISŘFA). The poor government official had actually thought he had scored a trip to India to meet the Indians. Chief Angus looked at one nephew who looked at his other nephew who looked at the remaining cousin who shrugged. The only comment the chief could make was a weary sigh.

The Kaaw Wiyaa seemed to be doing the Kaaw Wiyaa equivalent of a bow. "We come from 734 light-years away. We have travelled far to bring greetings to your people. You are not alone in the universe."

Chief Angus wasn't sure how to respond to that. This particular situation had not been part of any of his briefings at the Assembly of First Nations. He knew light-years were a good-sized distance to travel because he had watched a lot of *Star Trek* as a kid. Unlike Cheemo, he had always appreciated it more than *Star Wars*. He marvelled at the kind of travel allowance and per diem a trip in light-years must pull in. Seeing the gills on the Kaaw Wiyaa quiver as it spoke reminded the chief that he had a fairly large and tasty muskie fish back home in his freezer. He'd have to run home to defrost it in time for dinner.

Teddy, who was standing closest to the creature, could feel the alien's body heat coming off it in waves. Evidently, wherever it came from was a lot hotter than here. Add that to the smell of the Kaaw Wiyaa, the tightness of the room, and the fact they'd forgotten to bring the rest of the beer with them, and Teddy was feeling a bit woozy.

Tarzan had never been in the chief's office before. Surreptitiously, he pocketed two pens from his desk.

"We would like to open diplomatic relations with the people and government of Earth. That is why I am here."

The chief wondered if this was how the Beothuk and Mi'kmaq chiefs felt five hundred years ago. Wow, life is truly cyclical, he thought. The remnants of his activist youth (he'd gone to a protest once) resurfaced, and he restrained the urge to tell the large glowing, quivering, slimy thing in front of him to go home and leave his people alone. The reserve and the planet were all full up. But the pragmatic and diplomatic politician quickly reasserted itself. You don't get to be the former vice-chief for Central Ontario for the Assembly of First Nations without knowing a few things. Still, the man was at a loss as to how to proceed.

Outside his office door, the chief thought he heard Laurie, head of membership and lands, slip and fall with a loud and painful thud, probably on the trail of slime left by the problem standing in front of him. He'd better do something to get this thing out of the building before it triggered any lawsuits.

"As is protocol, our Grand Council has instructed me to request that you, as leader of this great planet, designate an ambassador to return with us to Kaaw Wiyaa to facilitate a cultural exchange and begin negotiations. As a goodwill gesture, we would be willing to construct sizable stone pyramids, or assist in the erection of enormous rock heads, or create giant stone circular calendars, as per your customs. We humbly await your decision."

Chief Angus was in a pickle, and he hated being in a pickle. None of those things would be of any use to Otter Lake. A decent water filtration system would be welcome, but he doubted this traveller from Kaaw Wiyaa would have the patience or the know-how to tackle the necessary forms and applications to navigate all the bureaucratic levels. Just the smell of the creature would probably fail the environmental assessment.

Ambassador... hmmm, thought the chief. In the corner, on the table, Tarzan sneezed. In the closed room, the smell was beginning to get to him. He smiled sheepishly. The chief had an idea—three of them, in fact.

* * *

Passing the orbit of Earth's moon, the Kaaw Wiyaa craft picked up speed as the quantum drive became fully operational. Soon, the Kaaw Wiyaa equivalent of a computer, buried somewhere deep in the ship, would calculate the best opportunity to open a space-time portal, taking the vessel back to its home. Behind the ship, the planet Earth was already fading into the distance, rapidly becoming just another speck of light in the spectacular backdrop of the universe. Tarzan, Cheemo and Teddy watched their home get smaller and smaller. Needless to say, they had mixed emotions about their recent appointment as ambassadors from Earth to the Kaaw Wiyaa Galactic Confederation. This was not how they had expected their day to end.

From the beginning, all three had doubts about Chief Angus's so-called "brilliant solution." Cheemo had never been out of the county or country, let alone the planet. Teddy got seasick, which is embarrassing enough when you come from a family of fishermen. There was no telling how space travel would affect him. And Tarzan needed the sound of purring from at least one of his three cats in order to fall asleep. They'd been on the ship for a little more than an hour, and there didn't seem to be any cats. Maybe this wasn't such a good idea, he thought. The other two were thinking the same thing, but ever since they were young, Chief Angus had been able to talk them into anything. Case in point.

As Otter Lake and Earth seemed to wink out in the distance, Tarzan had an afterthought. They should have brought some beer.

There were now four other members of the ship's crew standing—or whatever the Kaaw Wiyaa equivalent was—in the large pale-green room. There seemed to be more area on the inside of the ship than the three men had thought possible, based on what they saw of the exterior as they entered. Oh well, they decided to add this to the list of mysteries. Tricks like this would sure help with the housing shortage in their community.

"We are very honoured that you have accepted our offer to join us as representatives of your people. The citizens of Planet Earth must be very proud of you."

Teddy gave them his best 'ah shucks' shrug. Tarzan was barely conscious of the conversation. He was still looking out the window, wondering if it was too late to... literally... jump ship.

"If I may speak freely, what truly impressed us were your methods of communication. Metacommunication. Your ability to communicate without interacting verbally. Almost a form of telepathy. It was that ability that convinced us of your planet's sophistication."

All three men smiled, looking down at the mauve floor shyly, not really understanding what they were being complimented on.

"Please forgive us, we have misplaced our manners. Perhaps you would like something to drink?"

Tarzan nodded enthusiastically.

"We have something from our planet that you might find mildly intoxicating, based on what we know about human physiology. Would that be acceptable?"

The head Kaaw Wiyaa turned to one of the subordinate crew members and flopped a tentacle.

Once again, Tarzan nodded enthusiastically.

The crew member produced three two-foot tall containers that it delicately handed over to the beings from Earth. Each took one, noting how heavy it was. Tarzan examined his closely for any type of opening while

Cheemo sniffed at his. The aroma was not unpleasant, a cross between freshly cut grass and new-car smell.

Suddenly, Teddy's container jerked rather dramatically, as if something inside was trying to escape. Almost immediately, the same happened with the other two—a violent and agitated shift of weight. It reminded Tarzan of one of his cats trying to get out of its carrier. Teddy was just about to drop his when their host quickly cautioned them.

"Do not let it out. If it escapes, that will ruin the taste. Just hold it firmly, like this." Then the Kaaw Wiyaa lifted his up and quickly thudded it against the wall. The container stopped moving. "This stuns the main ingredient and enhances the flavour."

Cheemo, feeling almost adventurous in his new environment, gripped it fiercely and rammed his surprisingly sturdy container against the bulkhead. Not wanting to be outdone, the other two quickly copied. Now, all of them had ceased their frantic tremoring.

"Now drink," their host said, and raised its container to what all three Ojibway earthlings assumed was its mouth. At the top of the container, they noticed, was a small pyramid-shaped aperture. Then it tilted the drink back and seemed to swallow.

Encouraged, Teddy decided it would be rude not to at least sample their host's beverage. Conscious something was alive inside it, he tentatively tipped it back. The other two followed suit.

It was hard to describe the taste—peanut butter mixed with apple pie mixed with moose—but each felt he could definitely get used to it. It certainly wasn't beer, but there was an agreeable… what could only be described as *twinkling* in their nerve endings that came a few seconds after ingestion. All silently agreed they'd drunk worse.

Once more, whatever was inside Teddy's container gave a violent reaction, but by now, the experienced Teddy just held his drink firmly, thwacked it against the wall and the forceful shaking subsided.

Tarzan had already drained his and was holding it up, indicating he wouldn't mind a second. Before he could speak, he was presented with another one, already quivering with flavour. I could get used to this, he thought.

"We hope you will feel at home here."

Suddenly, the familiar couches they had been so comfortably ensconced on that morning were waiting behind them. They were sure they could smell the familiar breeze coming off the lake. The sound of the cicadas was back. And, by golly, there were even a few bushes scattered around the couches, with the old firepit in the middle. It was like they were back at Old Man's Point. "We have tried to replicate the environment we originally approached you in. We hope it is satisfactory, ambassadors from Earth."

Tarzan, Cheemo and Teddy each took another sip as they sat in their familiar seats. Getting comfortable on their favourite couches, all three nodded their heads in contentment. This ambassador thing might actually turn out okay. After all, they'd had worse jobs.

"We should have done this years ago," said Cheemo.

ACKNOWLEDGEMENTS

This book has had a long and exasperating gestation period. Ever since my first foray into writing occurred a thousand years ago, speculative fiction has held a special interest for me. Several times I have endeavoured to compile an anthology of Native sci-fi from Canada's best First Nations writers, but I was stymied repeatedly. The writers were more than willing to expand the boundaries of what was considered Aboriginal literature. But because of the annoying fact that writers want to get paid, and as a writer/anthologist myself I wanted to damn well pay them, it proved financially difficult to get a book like that off the ground. Add to that the novelty aspect of something called Native science fiction and the grey area it had sprung from, and it was too much of an unknown commodity for some publishers. At least twice my dream fell by the wayside. But, to quote a saying, resistance is futile.

So, partially out of frustration, "Well, screw it. I'll do it myself," I found myself saying. Here stands the final product. In a blitz of enthusiasm and creativity, I wrote six of the stories in a two-month period during a lazy fall. The rest followed at a more relaxed pace over the winter.

There are many people who have been there to encourage me during this drawn-out phase of creation. First and foremost, to all the Aboriginal writers out there who I have contacted several times over the last ten years trying to put this together and whom, in the end, I had to disappoint. This common interest we shared gave me the impetus to actually put this together myself. Live long and prosper, you all.

To Dan David—my Mohawk adviser, whom I secretly believe to be a Morlock; Trish Rody—my medical adviser, who just may be an Eloi; Marianne Nicolson, who "phoned home" for me; and finally, Alvin Chacko—my computer Jedi. Thank you for sharing your wisdom.

Institutionally, this book could not have happened without a writing grant from the Ontario Arts Council. Also, a stint as a writer-in-residence for Wilfrid Laurier University provided me with the time and resources to finish this book. Both organizations kept me in Soma and Soylent Green while I wrote this.

You would not be reading this if it wasn't for the crew at Douglas & McIntyre and my editor, Shirarose Wilensky, who all believed that Indians could fly (metaphorically speaking, of course). Thank you for seeing the possibilities. May the Force be with you.

And of course, my biggest thank you to my inspiration, Janine Willie, upon whose resources, love and patience I have relied extensively. I grok you.

Meegwetch, and always remember—in a writer's office, no one can hear you scream.

DREW HAYDEN TAYLOR

Note: To members of the Kwakwaka'wakw Nation and any academics who might want to Google the stories of the Impatient One and others I mentioned in Mr. Gizmo, you needn't bother. They don't exist. I made them up. It's not my usual practice to make up another nation's cultural stories. In fact, it goes against my Indigenous nature and under normal circumstances could be considered very bad manners. However, this situation, heavily flavoured with irony, required it.

In writing the story, I wanted to be truthful and accurate to the Kwakwaka'wakw people. My partner is Kwakwaka'wakw. Therefore, I sought direction from her cousin regarding traditional stories about inanimate objects that come to life or speak. After receiving several emails full of information, I incorporated much of what was relayed to me into the story.

Still wanting to be respectful and accurate, I sent my cultural contact the completed short story to make sure I hadn't committed any cultural faux pas. Evidently I had. A major one. I was promptly told, on the very day I had to send my completed manuscript to my publisher, that all the stories I had been told were not to be used by me in any fashion. In Kwakwaka'wakw culture, many stories are considered "cultural property," owned by a particular family or community. The information I was sent had been meant only as an example for personal reference and could not be included in my story under any circumstances. A rather unique dilemma.

So, in the end, I was forced to create legends of my own to fill out the context of Mr. Gizmo and not be disrespectful to my girlfriend's people by using particulars. If I have offended anybody, my apologies.

Sometimes being a respectful Native writer can be peculiar.

ABOUT THE AUTHOR

Drew Hayden Taylor is an award-winning playwright, novelist, scriptwriter and journalist. He was born and raised on the Curve Lake First Nation in Central Ontario. Taylor has authored nearly thirty books, including *The Night Wander: A Native Gothic Novel* (Annick, 2007) about an Anishinabe vampire. He also edited *Me Funny*, *Me Sexy* and *Me Artsy* (Douglas & McIntyre, 2006, 2008 and 2015), and has been nominated for two Governor General's Awards. He lives in his community.